HER LEGACY

Readers 18+++

LEANA TAYLOR

Malherbe Publishers Publication
Author: Leana Taylor
Book cover: Malherbe Publishers
Set in Franklin Gothic Book 12pt

First Edition 2025
Copyright ©Leana Taylor
ISBN 978-1-991455-77-2

For seven years I braved my cuffs of emotional abuse.
I wanted it to be love but it never was.
Now, seven years later,
I am celebrating my emancipation.

"Diamonds on the soles of her shoes" from the album Graceland (1986) by Paul Simon.

"She's a rich girl
she don't try to hide it
diamonds on the
soles of her shoes

he's a poor boy
empty as a pocket
empty as a pocket with
nothing to lose"

OVERTURE

5 June 1832. The Galway Hooker, named "The Banshee", started out on a choppy sea late afternoon but the waves calmed gradually as the sun started to set. Now, the crescent moon faintly smeared the side of the 13,5-meter-long fishing boat, illuminating the way.

It was a clear night, for the moment, but fog would settle down before sunrise. According to the captain's calculations, they had fifty kilometres ahead, but he was not concerned. He smiled, lovingly patted the old, worn, ship's wheel and stared straight ahead.

He had an unusual cargo on board: a woman of considerable means, accompanied by another female friend, both guarded by five unarmoured knights but for swords in their sheaths. The ladies' faces were veiled when they were brought by cart, and stayed veiled as they climbed into the dinghy and got rowed to the waiting boat. Both greeted him respectfully, although they kept their eyes averted.

The old Skipper recalled the previous journey, and to his reckoning it had to have been twenty years before. It was none of his business why they were headed to Lone Peak.

What a treacherous place! An old castle sitting high upon the cliffs with no obvious way to reach it. Legend had it that nobody lived there because it was haunted. But, just like the first time, he had repeated an oath of secrecy. His household had never wanted for anything since the two lads of the Secret Society approached him years ago and he had proved his reliability ever since. He had gotten old, with fewer teeth, a bald head and soddy lungs, but his heart stayed loyal.

The Banshee had a steady wind tonight and the crimson sails puffed like a young women's breasts. "Aye!" he sighed, pulling his woollen cap tighter over his ears, before re-lighting his pipe. After a satisfied grunt, he resumed his thoughts with his hand loosely on the wheel. "What would the lads make of it?" He watched the tobacco smoke drifting uncertainly before the breeze swept it into darkness.

His friends were all anglers like him; hookers. They went by this name because of the method of fishing they used, dragging lines with bait on hooks through the water. Their boats were all Galway's, named after the Irish Bay, they originated from. They were the best there was, sturdy, dependable beasts fitted with calico sails, unbleached, not fully processed cotton. They were covered in a solution of tree bark, tar and butter which made them weatherproof and gave them the reddish, rusty brown colour.

"They would never believe it, anyway!" he chuckled, reaching automatically for his hipflask he had dutifully left at home for this trip. "Better be sharp! Sharp, Captain!" he snorted, embarrassed when he realized one of the unarmoured knights had appeared like an apparition out of thin air, staring at him. "It would not do to swim with the fish at this, or any hour!" he added a little nervously.

In the lower deck, in the space between the gently creaking ribs of the vessel, Aine sat wide awake. They were comfortable enough; the silent routine of the knight's shifts did not bother her at all. A thin curtain was hung midway which gave the two ladies privacy. Next to her, Bridget was fast asleep on the mattress they shared. "Today is my fifty-fourth birthday," she reflected, "an old maid!" Aine smiled. She did a quick calculation as she stroked Bridgette's hair. "She is only thirty," Aine thought, "and I cannot see life without her!"

Aine had a fleeting thought of the mansion she had left behind and recalled the schedule for the evening visitors. There was nothing to worry about. She missed the merriment of the regulars around the dinner table and the lazy evenings when they were all draped over a sofa, sometimes naked. Gertrude and her husband, Johann, would be there, and Sylvia and Francois. Bahati from East Africa was their favourite, with her full lips and luxuriously soft, dark skin. When the morning dawned, they would eventually find their partners and return home while Bahati slept peacefully on the floor in her room, like her culture dictated.

There were no windows in the hold, but they kept the hatch open. Through it, moonlight fell silkily on the stairs. On a small, low table were the remnants of their meal -fresh olive bread, butter, grapes, tomatoes, nuts, sliced cucumber, cheese, dates, dried apricots and apples. Red wine in a glass tumbler and a pitcher of fresh water. Compliments of The Manor kitchen.

They had long since grown accustomed to the faint smell of fish, lingering even after the boat had been in dry dock for nearly three months, a period spent trying to rid it of the odor while preparing the specially lowered deck.

The captain was handsomely reimbursed for his lack of income by faking an injured arm. Of course, the preparations were excessive but necessary. Their safety depended on them being inconspicuous and, besides, the journey inland would take much longer and the perils were much higher.

Aine shifted her weight and let Bridget settle again in her lap. She lay her head back against the rough wood, feeling the gentle vibrations of the vessel and closed her eyes. Unbeknownst to her, she would become the great, great, great, great grandmother of a pretty lady called Jana centuries later and Jana would also have a daughter.

Sleep came to her at last. The gathering she had been summoned to, was especially important; the signing ceremony of the Jene Turaq, or Ten Rules. As an ancestor of the ancient Celtic family Donchadh, the founding family of the elite Secret Society of Revered Ladies, she would be the first to receive a copy. The Society stemmed from a splinter of a Catholic sect and were severely condemned by the church. She had lost both her parents in an uprising when she was younger. Luckily, her grandmother was saved and had brought her up.

The captain gently touched the helm to readjust their course. The Hooker cleaved a clean line through the dark water, scattering white foam in her wake, shaking off the touch of the crescent moon as if in irritation. Dawn would break in three hours; he could sense the thick fog forming on the surface of the icy water. The return journey would be much the same. He perked up because he would meet old friends at the docking area to exchange laughter and smokes with and to enjoy the festive meal he knew was waiting for them on the small sandy beach. There would be no drinking though, under the watchful eyes of the ever-present knights.

They were not to be toyed with; they were hardened men who would sacrifice their lives to protect these women. The captain knew they had females too who functioned as custodians, either as part of the households or else did service as cleaners and cooks. Some of these women were hardened by difficult circumstances such as poverty and abuse. Once they were offered a better life in the employ of these homesteads, they stayed loyal and protective to the point of worship.

Aine had reddish brown hair, worn long and, for this occasion, weaved and pinned around her head in an intricate pattern. She had escaped the burly build of her Viking ancestors although her physical strength and skills with a bow and arrow were legendary. Bridget, her niece, on the other hand, was comely, plump, and kind. She had apple-red cheeks, a button nose and a soft, gurgling laugh against her own milky white complexion, sharper nose, and often uninviting features.

The ladies were woken up by the gentle voice of one of the knights. They had arrived and had a little time to freshen up. He gestured to a bowl of steaming water and fresh towels. He respectfully withdrew as did the remaining men downstairs. The hatch shut with a thud, momentarily dumping the space in darkness before two oil lamps painted their part of the hull in fiery reds and yellows. The waves gently bumped against the sides of the boat.

Mullach Singilte. Lone peak. She did not need to see it to recall the imposing structure in her mind's eye. Bridget stretched lazily before she gave Aine a soft kiss on her mouth. "Better get ready," she whispered.

Aine smiled and got to her feet, slowly undressing. "It is much colder here," she realized when her body was rid of her clothes, "I am so happy Bridget made me take my fur coat!" While Bridget helped her wash, her thoughts drifted with the soft strokes of the sponge over her body.

The signing of the Jene Turaq would be witnessed by the highest overseers, represented by three women of three generations; Roisin (83), Cara (44) and Deidre (28). The knights would be represented by the three highest orders; Fergal, Cormac and Caibre. The compilation of the rules had taken a long time since they were so vital and were meant to be adhered to, forever. The founder of the elite Secret Society of Revered Ladies (SSORL) was Arynn Argall Donchadh, Aine recalled her mother telling her.

Contrary to belief, he had not built the castle, although he did live and die in it.

"Well, look at you, my lady!" Bridget said, admiring Aine in her robe of the darkest green, with silver trim around the neckline and cuffs.

"Thank you, my sweet," Aine answered, as a discreet knock on the hatch told her the time of departure was near. She would go alone while two knights stayed behind with Bridget. She snuggled into her fur coat when the hatch opened. The chilly air took her breath away, as did the sheer rock walls of the peak.

The fog blurred the world around her, and she nearly stumbled on the slick deck. Her brow furrowed irritably. Faraway she could hear thunder. Two knights gallantly appeared on either side, offering their arms to steady her.

The Banshee was closer to shore than she thought and through the mist she could make out other, similar vessels. They were docked in a small, protected bay.

A misty rain started to fall as she was rowed to shore. Small waves bravely broke and dived beneath the dinghy, giving it forward momentum. She could hear men's voices, but it sounded disembodied. It must be the skippers, she realized, assembled somewhere on the shore.

Aine was guided along a narrow stone pathway, sheltered beneath a tarp held over her head. It amplified the sound of the rain and the cold. A donkey stood tethered where the steep incline started. There was not a visible path to follow; it looked like nothing more but a hair fracture in the massive rock structure. The going was slow but steady as the donkey was lead upwards while she covered her head with the tarp that was offered to her. She could hear the footfall of the knight behind her and the metallic sound of his sword's sheath against the rock surface. Around corners she thought she could hear other donkeys and the faint drifting of rising and falling voices.

It looked impossible to reach the castle; all they could see when she dared peek, was an endless, solid wall. It felt like hours. Then, suddenly the rain stopped, and a watery sun appeared just as the donkey gave one final push to clear the incline. There, not a hundred meters further, stood the castle. Here, up high, a new sound could be heard; the crashing of tall waves against the sides of Mullach Singilte.

She had been here once before, and it was a visit she never forgot because the magnitude of it was so large. Two knights, dressed in full armour, had willingly sacrificed their lives by stepping off the enormous cliffs, with a haversack of rocks tied to their backs for extra weight. There was no forgiveness for their ineptitude in protecting her parents. It had not mattered that the murderers were identified and their throats slit in a dark alley. All the recruited knights knew the weight of their failure and when the burden became too much, there was an honourable way out. They were not the first.

Aine wished her grandmother had not forced her to witness it. What good did it do? But she was too young to protest. The nightmares kept her awake, the precision with which they stepped over the cliff, the lack of any visible emotion, the glint of the sun on the helmets and the tragic wave of their plumes as they disappeared. She imagined that they turned into seagulls, to lessen the pain and the guilt she felt. It was said that rusted armour often washed out on the beach, sometimes still with the skeletal limb it once protected inside.

Escorted on both sides by the knights, their shoes clicked on the stone path that led to the front door. Behind them, she made out the sound of other visitors about to clear the last incline. It was by no means a beautiful place. She would rather describe it as "imposing" and even "dreadful" and not because of its size, but its height and the numerous turrets sticking out like sore teeth. It looked ominous even from afar. The ancient stone blocks of its body, darkened by age and the salty air, were smaller in size compared to others she had seen. Rumour had it that it was due to the difficulty of the building site; the smaller blocks were easier to manage since they arrived by boat and got hauled up the cliff with a pulley system. It was also said that many a man and beast had lost their lives before the castle was completed and it would therefore always be haunted.

Now, moss and algae were growing on the surface, attempting to hide its shame. One would expect a certain foul odour around castles; a combination of poorly discarded food, animal and human waste, vermin, unwashed bodies and the dampness and mustiness that married it. The lack of stink was because not many residents occupied the castle regularly.

Her reminiscing stopped. Seagulls called for their mates in the mist, sending a shiver up her spine. Two huge wooden doors swung open noiselessly, eerily displaying the forecourt which was brightly lit by the sun. It felt pleasantly warm here; protected. She smiled as a knight took her coat.

Eleven chairs were set in two rows before a raised platform. It was the set of an especially important tradition. The youngest knight, who was often no older than eighteen, was tasked with reciting the founding principles of the Secret Society of Revered Ladies from memory. It was an enormous honour that would not easily be forgotten and many of his equals would never have the opportunity to perform.

Gentlemen, which she knew were in various professions and had sworn an oath to belong to the Secret Society, appeared to escort the ladies, who respectfully waited their turn in line behind her.

"Miss Aine Donchadh," a pleasant voice said, guiding her by her elbow to a chair in the front row. "What a pleasure! Welcome!" He reverted to Argallah, the secret language.

Aine relaxed. She was home here. She accepted his offer of some chilled wine, surprised by the option since ice was harvested during wintertime and stored in an icehouse. It was a rare luxury for this out-of-place castle to have. She also acknowledged, since no trouble had been spared, the severity of the occasion.

Aine looked around her and greeted faces with a nod and a smile, which everybody returned. It was not as if they all knew each other, maybe just of each other! She smiled, thinking of the rampant gossip that would undoubtedly follow the function. They were not rivals, they were allies but they were still human, and they were all women and ladies liked to chatter!

"Lady Aine Donchadh," a woman of about her age greeted, extending her hand. "What a pleasure to meet you!" Introductions were made, greetings and salutations exchanged, and a soothing hum of voices, ranging through a wide age spectrum, filled the space.

The men in attendance, with beverages on offer, completed a picture postcard - a Mary Cassatt painting where the stout pillars that supported the canopy over the platform was draped with lianas with healthy green leaves. Vases of wildflowers were masterfully placed to catch the eye and draw the admirer into a peaceful slumber.

Then a gentleman appeared on the platform, immediately changing the aura of the room from a festive gathering to a formal occasion. "Ladies," he spoke, as silence fell; twenty-two eyes riveted upon him. He spoke Argallah fluently and with respect. "Welcome! Let us start the proceedings. Without further ado, our founding principles will now be recited by our youngest knight, as forerunner to the formal function."

The young knight stepped forward, his chainmail a size too big, holding his head high. He looked angelic, with curly blonde hair and soft stubble on his cheeks. He had blue eyes and freckles, the arm on which his helmet rested, steady. Aine saw him clench his free hand into a fist, loosen it and with a clear, strong voice started his oration.

His voice rose clear and forceful, echoing off the surrounding walls. His eyes briefly came to rest on hers, her seating indicating her status. She gave him a reassuring smile. Satisfied, she saw a faint blush cover his cheeks.

"Arynn Argall Donchadh, the founder of the elite Secret Society of Revered Ladies, was a great believer in the manumission of women's sexual needs. He was a gentleman of extensive means. He believed the church oppressed their free will by misinterpreting the Scripture and ensuing unfair, harsh punishment and even imposed the death sentence unfairly. His aim was to establish a safe and secure environment for distinguished women to practise and explore, free from fear, ridicule, and prosecution. This," and here the brave young man swallowed briefly, "sets these women and their practices apart from common brothels."

Aine heard the distant rumble of thunder once more, but this time it seemed closer. She dreaded being there when the storm hit. Lightning would strike the building without mercy, and heavy rain would batter its walls like stones.

The knight resumed his oration. His voice had a pleasant lilt to it that made his words interesting. Aine wondered which part of the world he originated from.

"Mister Donchadh befriended like-minded, powerful individuals he trusted. Amongst them were married men who supported their wives, protected them, and indulged in the activities themselves.

Argallah, the secret language, was founded to communicate the existence of the elite Secret Society and also to identify establishments which wished for protection. A percentage of its revenue was due to the society. The owners, of course, stayed the main overseers and how they managed it, was up to them.

"Born out of these sprouted the true embodiment of the houses; women's bodies are their holy grail, and it is meant to be revered and worshipped by those who visited. All the ladies could furthermore choose a pseudonym if they wished to. Together, Arynn and his friends became the founding members of the elite Secret Society who recruited other sworn supporters in various fields that were tasked with forming an impenetrable shell of legal jargon with supported documentation no authority could override."

Aine loved the next section and by the looks of anticipation on the other ladies' faces. The feeling was mutual.

"Being a ladies' man himself," he continued with an appropriate smile in his voice, "Arynn wished for the hereditary continuation of these establishments where the daughters of ladies stood in direct lineage to inherit an establishment. To be successful and to fulfil his desire for chivalry, Arynn Argall harvested knights who did either temporary or full-time service while continuing their training. These hardened men are always present but inconspicuous around the houses, under the watchful eyes of a designated senior. They are the true protectors who carry the cross of the order of the Celtic Knights upon their chests. Failure is not tolerated. It is punishable by death."

He uttered these words proudly and with a raised voice to be heard over the thunder.

"Over the course of a few years, the Wall of Admissions was introduced which records the details of prospective visitors and their history. Any person found lacking, for whatever reason which does not need to be shared, would be refused entry."

"The Jene Turaq now forms the supporting pillar for the Wall of Admissions. Failure to adhere to it is punishable by death. It will be signed on this historical day and be an unwavering document."

He paused before delivering the last sentence.

"What a sad day not to have Mister Arynn Argall Donchadh present. We honour his legacy."

As if by magic, a bright ray of sunshine pierced through the clouds like a sword and lit up Lone Peak like a beacon as the last words were spoken.

(Image from Pinterest)

19 October 1900. Seaports had long been hubs for everything that arrived from or departed to the sea. In addition to port authorities, customs, fish auctions, packing facilities, large shipping companies, and the import/export trade, they also met the demand for sex. For the widowed or unmarried women along the coast, it often became a harsh struggle for survival.

The Anglo-Boer war was in full swing and the ports of entry were busy. Both the ships and trains needed coal and troops flooded the piers on their way to and back from various stations. Most of the young men habitually visited some of the "institutions of ill repute" in cul-de-sac alleys where a strange merriment, fuelled by alcohol, prevailed. They were known as "red light" districts where law enforcement was relaxed and even officers of the cloth had a favourite girl! The colour red signalled "danger" as much as it persuaded. Many dangerous, slippery and poorly lit back porch steps recognised the boots it led to barred back doors. A few coins and a bit of paper money exchanged hands and everyone was welcome.

Captain Shawn Smit finished smoking his cigarette and flicked the butt over the pier where it instantly died as it hit the water. His skin was tingling from the harsh soap he had washed with. He was turned out smartly, dressed in a clean uniform, shiny shoes, a dash of "Ol' English Leather" cologne on his pulse, and his hair was combed back with a cheeky fringe. He had a smile on his lips and a song in his heart - a dashing young man looking forward to a pleasant evening. His transport was waiting just out of sight of the crowds.

"Sunset," he thought, whistling a tune softly. "A whole evening to enjoy!" Shawn was admitted to the elite Secret Society after his application had been approved. All the higher-ranking officers could apply but not everyone was accepted.

This was his second visit to the Bastion. He softly murmured the Jene Turaq as he climbed into the waiting horse-drawn cart. *"Xo chatè; xo prokè, xo qabra, xo vowrè, xo micotè, xo shakrè, xo commeta, xo telmè, pratè xo paca and xo barenè."*

27 August 1924. There is a straggling old house in a cul-de-sac on a sandy hill in a village called Gonubie. A sun-bleached name board hanging on a rusted baton declares the dwelling's name to be "The Bastion". The wind takes care not to rattle the loose roof tiles too much, let the numerous sandstorms swirl graciously past and when a thunderstorm threatens, let the fervor of it loose over the sea and village first. It is tender with the house, showing it mercy as if it feels sorry for it, and why shouldn't it? It has withstood many years of onslaughts; it looks worn out, old and cranky but it stubbornly clings to its foundations, determined not to collapse.

It had not always been like this. The Bastion used to be a lively place with a long and colorful history reaching back to earlier generations and mistresses with riches untold. Like the darkened windows and firmly shut doors, it also hid a secret and a legacy which was firmly sustained under the cover of the forgotten address. Like a dead tree stump which maintains a world of bugs under its torso; giving it shelter, making it flourish while its body is slowly destroyed by the very bugs seeking its protection. But everything was not as it seemed...

(Image from Pinterest)

CHAPTER 1

12 September 1932. Jana Duncan closed the glass cabinet's door, securing the lock. She could see the framed document through the glass, standing in the center of the second shelf. It looked like some sort of certificate with a printed gold leave border and calligraphy writing. "These are the unbreakable rules," her mother had told her. "There are no excuses and no exceptions. Not ever. The language is our own but must be clarified to everybody who visits. It must be signed and sworn upon."

She was made to learn them, by heart. She whispered them on her way up the stairs to her bedroom: *"The Jene Turaq."*

"Xo chatè; xo prokè, xo qabra, xo vowrè, xo micotè, xo shakrè, xo commeta, xo telmè, pratè xo paca and xo barenè."

The ten rules. If she closed her eyes, she could conjure up her mothers' image as she spoke to her that day. "It is not 'just rules' Jana and it may sound simple, but it embraces many complications. It has been handed down from mother to daughter for as long as I can remember. Blood has flown and mini wars fought over it. Without it, there are no limits. If you are outside of it, there is no return. That is survival."

1

She knew she would inherit The Bastion, as her mother had before her. Jana never questioned it, it was her inheritance and she intended to keep it to the best of her ability until she, too, could pass it on to her daughter. Their big, old house sounded quiet, but she had a trained ear and knew it was only because of the heavy wooden doors. If she looked closely where the old wooden floors sagged a little, she could tell where the films were being shot because of the lighting used and the soft burr of the video cameras.

There was hardly a day without guests. She could tell who was behind every closed door, she could go in if she wanted to. There was no need to announce herself in any way but there was time enough for visiting later.

Jana was twelve years old, and she could not wait to experience what she had seen. "Four years from now, when I'm sixteen, it's not a lifetime and I will be called Lilly," she had finally decided, extremely excited.

CHAPTER 2

Present day.

"School sucks, Adelaide!" Jean is saying. We are walking home under a sun hot on our school blazers; we are under extremely strict orders not to be seen without them, except in class. "You know what his ex-girlfriend told me? Well, anyway! He made it clear that he wanted me instead!"

I am only half listening. Truth be told, I am not living in the same world as they are. Every day is a pretense. Most of the time I succeed quite well in faking it but today is not one of them. Luckily for me Jean is not paying me much attention because Benjamin has finally got round to asking her to be his girlfriend. Any other friend would have shared her excitement, and I feel like a fake friend for only giving her less than half of my attention. I wish I could tell her things, and I wish she would understand, but I cannot.

We near her house. My schoolbag's strap is digging into my shoulder; it is so heavy! Jean is too smitten to notice the irritation I know is written all over my face; the involuntary twitch across my brow always gives me away. Jean is my closest and only friend; she has known me since we were in grade one. Our parents are only acquaintances, and we do not visit each other's homes. Jean has endured so much ridicule because of our friendship, it boggles my mind that she stays friends with me. She is still blabbering away happily and ends abruptly with a "Anyway! See you!" giving me a kiss on my cheek before she skips home.

"Okay! See you!" I call after her, smiling to myself. How foolish people are when they fall in love!

My house is not far; just up the incline and to the left at the end of the short cul-de-sac: The Bastion. It is an old, spacious house with two stories and it has been in my mother's family for generations. Most of the windows face the ocean. The high surrounding walls came up before I was born, which is quite recent for a place this old! The Bastion has its history meticulously recorded; it is well known to me. It used to have a red light illuminating the slippery steps that lead from the beach to the back door.

I punch in my code at the electronic gate which slides open and close. *Maria Madeline*, the tiny, purple, climbing rose is in full bloom, she snakes up the pillars leading to the front door. She has a sweet, almost nauseating smell in the still heat of the day. There is the sound of waves breaking, a comforting sound. In the shade at our front door, I drop my schoolbag and let my blazer fall over it. I want to pull off my shoes too but keep them on because the paving stones around the house will be scorching.

It is incredibly quiet. In the garages at the back is my father's black Mercedes; he is a medical doctor, and my mother's smaller Porsche. She is a qualified translator. Then there are the other vehicles - a run-down motorcycle, a Mini Cooper van, a blue Jaguar, a white SUV parked in the sun and Ludwick's red convertible under the tree, as usual. It is still upsetting not seeing the scooter next to the garages, but it will pass; "One's first always has a special place," my mother told me. I quicken my step; if I manage my time right, I can still have a quick swim before my session.

CHAPTER 3

I still have my monthly cycle; everything is scheduled around the dates when I am clear. It is very punctual; my father says it is a good thing. "We'll only interfere when you're older, love," he said in his serious voice. I feel excited because I have just finished my cycle and that means a blissful three weeks to enjoy myself.

My room is as spacious as my parents'—the soft light of dusk filters through the window, casting an ethereal fog-like glow. As I apply my makeup, my reflection mirrors that of my parents: their blue eyes, my father's brown hair that curls when wet, and his full lips. We all share a slender build and tall stature—I stand at 1.72 meters. My love for swimming, instilled by my mother, Jana, traces back to the earliest days of my life when she taught me to swim as soon as I could walk.

My parents do not share my photogenic memory; they are a little jealous of it! I do not really have to study, which helps with my academic subjects but unfortunately, I still must do my assignments, which involve notes and typing, and it takes time.

I wonder what plans Jean and Benjamin will concoct to see each other; it is a weekday and Jean's parents will not allow her to go out. Benjamin could slip out; such things are easier for boys. Mark used to too. He jokingly said he could slip through any burglar barred window like a ghost! Only my father knew his background and his medical health; compulsory information he kept in his cabinet, which was quite full. I was lucky to have him; he was older and experienced and when he whispered that he would not hurt me, he kept his promise.

There's still time left; I do not have to dress because I do not need to. Night has come, the sky glittering with stars. My window is opened to the breeze and the moonlight, I decide to sit in the murkiness because it is so peaceful, and let my thoughts roam. I recall the image of my parents making love, the first time I was brought in to see them. They spoke to me in hushed voices, but I was not scared. My father would catch his breath after kissing and say, "We use our tongues, love. It turns lovers on." I was tutored since I was twelve and instructed not to be shy about my body or sex. "Didn't God give us this gift? Why should we not enjoy it?" they would laugh.

I have seen them many times and not always with each other. Ludwick was with my mother a lot. "My Lilly," he would croon in her ear and together they would climax, shuddering under the hot studio lights and in full view of the bored camera staff, traipsing around the bed on their bare feet with their recording gear for a better angle, a better shot. I would be careful not to get in their way.

There is the soft knock on my bedroom door. It is time for me to go. I can never tell anyone about any of it. My parents are paying astronomical amounts to lawyers to safeguard our house. There's also my mother's family; an ancient and prestigious lineage with mysterious ways and influence undreamed of. It would be my business one day. It has sound rules and here everyone who is doing business is protected. Here I am called Tracy. It is the name I chose, like my mother chose Lilly as hers.

CHAPTER 4

They are waiting for me after school - Jacques de Kok, and his cronies. I hear them talking excitedly, too loud, and I sense trouble. I am alone and at present on a bend in the road out of the school's sight; the nearest houses are a street away. I glance behind me; the meeting was timed because I am alone on the road. It is going to rain soon; the clouds have been gradually gathering throughout the day and I did not bring an umbrella. I am in quite a hurry to get home.

"Hey, look whom we have here! Isn't it Adelaide Duncan?" Jacques is saying, taking a pull on the cigarette he is clumsily clamping between his fingers. I want to laugh at his show of nonchalance but realize just in time that it will anger him to be belittled in front of his friends standing uncertainly behind him. They avoid eye contact and busy themselves studying their shoes. Perhaps there's nothing to worry about, I think, trying to pass them.

"Hey!" he growls just as I am past him. He grabs my arm hard and pulls me close to him. Jacques has brown eyes, bad breath and the beginnings of stubble on his chin. He pushes himself up against me, I can feel his excitement. I can hear the thunder far off. There is a frigid wind blowing in from the ocean, ruffling the hair on the back of my head.

I keep my body slack, trying not to tense up. Some animal instinct argues that if I do, I will make my fear palpable. He is still uncertain since I still have not uttered a word.

"We don't like your kind around here," he says darkly. His friends look more out of place than ever. This gives me an advantage over him.

"Your pants shout something else!" I say with confidence, loud enough for his friends to hear, knowing full well that it is his worst moment. I am right. Two of the other boys' snigger at him.

Jacques' face turns scarlet before he pushes me away from him. "You're useless!" he shouts at them before he returns his attention to me. He let go of my arm just as the first raindrops come down over us. His plan did not pan out as he envisioned and he is at a loss. It makes him angrier. "Get the hell out of here!" he shouts at his friends without turning his head.

"Run!" my mind instructs my legs which are frozen to the spot. "Run! Damn you!" it resends the message, but my legs stay unresponsive. The rain is pelting down on us, soaking me through to my skin. "Buddy?" one of the boys reacts, "cool it, okay? What are you going to do?"

"What you are too lousy to do!" he answers softly, keeping his attention on me, his back to them. His face is contorted with rage now, water running over it and still I am frozen to the spot. His friends turn around, heading away from us. "You dig your own grave, Jacques! This was not part of the plan!" the same one who spoke to him, said. Their steps quicken as they start running.

My mouth is dry. I know what rape is. I am certain it is what he plans. Then he jumps at me, taking me completely by surprise. We roll down the side of the road, through the grass and the mud. I loose my schoolbag in the process and one of my shoes comes off.

We are rolling. He is hurting me where he grabbed hold of me. It is a minute before I come to my senses. We have stopped rolling. I can see the grey sky, the thunderclouds and the rivers of water ceaselessly coming down. I dare to move; I do not see Jacques. Then his face appears above me, blood running from a cut above his brow, mixed with the rain. He has a knife in his hand, raised. In seconds it is coming down, I try to roll away from him. There is a sharp, searing pain close to my hip. My face is buried in the filth, and it feels like I have lost all my strength. I could not care anymore. I only want him to be gone. I only want to be left alone.

CHAPTER 5

I can smell lavender and lemons and feel the gentle stroke of a sponge on my brow. Dare I open my eyes?

"Shsss, Sweet." It is my mother's voice. "You're safe now."

I fight the urge to slink back into sleep, opening one of my eyes slowly. I am in my bed; the light is too sharp so that I must squint. I feel my mother getting off my bed and hear her closing the curtains. She returns, smiling as she sits down again, taking my hand.

"How are you feeling?"

My throat feels raw when I try to speak, I must swallow first. "Like a train hit me." A tear glides down my mother's cheek, she does not try to hide it.

"I'm sorry," she says, "It is the one thing I have always dreaded more than anything. But I am grateful that he did not..." she stops, forced to by her crying. I give her hand a squeeze. She composes herself and takes a breath. "Daddy saw your schoolbag lying on the side of the road, so he stopped and called your name. You did not answer, then he saw you... When he ran in with you, limp in his arms, I wanted to die." The tears are coming again. "You have a nasty stab wound just below your hipbone. It's an ugly cut with ragged edges and thankfully it didn't go as deep as to damage your organs." My mother keeps very still, then continues, "your large intestine, appendix, colon, ureter, fallopian tubes or ovaries." She sighs, "But you'll carry the nasty scar forever."

I am hurting.

"Mom?"

She lets go of my hand and feels my temperature with the back of her hand.

"It was Jacques," I say to her.

"Yes, we found out, Sweet," she answers. "Rest now, okay, we must get that fever broken. I will bring you some lemonade."

I hear her leaving my room, bumping into my father as he is coming up the stairs. "She's awake," I hear, "but barely." I keep my eyes closed but manage to smile.

"There's my girl!" he beams like I knew he would." "I'm sorry, Love," he says, "You know I will kill the dragon for my family, don't you?"

I give myself a few seconds before I ask, "Did you, Dad?" There is silence; the house is devoid of people, it may be the first time in an exceptionally long time.

"No. I did not have to, Love. Shortly after I found you, I got a call. It was Darryl, Jacques' friend. He bawled the whole tale, in between crying and choking on his snot. His father slapped him. He is a nasty man. Working as a jail warden, he does not know gentle. A search party was organized to look for Jacques. He must have staggered too close to the rising river and fallen in. When they found him, it was too late."

I had been found four days before. Four days I know nothing about.

CHAPTER 5

East London is a large seaside city and the closest port of call to Goudie. The inland harbor is fed and sustained by the Gonubie River, which runs through our village and eventually spills out into the ocean.

We are driving in the SUV; we have two containers filled with X rated movies. To prying eyes, we are waiting to offload caviar to a luxury yacht which will be moored at the marina. I was given "special leave" by my father to accompany Charl with the delivery for two reasons; although I was sound in body and mind after my experience, my father recommended some off time and the delivery contained three films in which I appeared, for the first time. Our films have a set clientele, and we deliver as per order. Our films are laden with a whopping thirty-three percent tax on top of our selling price, which is never questioned. Our brand name always means quality and our customers know it.

We are early but the activities on the dock are already in full swing. It is a cool morning; it will turn out to be a sweltering day. Charl is staring across the harbor, his thoughts miles away and I do not feel talkative either. The yacht we are waiting for is called Namaste. She will dock in about fifty minutes' time, which is the last communication we received from her over the radio; all we must do is wait. He is one of our largest distributors, Mister Khan, who boasts that he has an exceptionally large private collection.

I feel protected because I know that Charl carries a weapon and as docile as he seems, will not hesitate to use it if he recognizes the need to. Of course, I was told about the unpredictability of men; I am to stay put when the delivery is made because if I am recognized, I may not be safe because I now have a monetary value. I have reached film star status.

How do I feel about Jacques? I am glad. I am glad he is dead. I wonder about Mark; where he is and what he is up to. He wanted to go to the United States to study but he did not have the money. "That's why I answered your advertisement," he drawled, his hair stubbornly falling into his eyes. He had curly hair, green eyes, soft lips, and a calm voice.

We were alone. He was going to be my first and it was not going to be filmed. "You're such a very lovely girl," he said when he started kissing me. He removed my bra when I asked him how many girls he had slept with. He smiled, he had beautiful teeth, even and white. "I've committed a few crimes," he smiled, caressing my nipples, "but 'none as lovely as you!"

I 'remember how turned on I was. I was moist and wanted him inside of me, badly. He let me touch him, showed me how to stroke it, slowly. He had his hand on me and did wonderful things with it, teasing me by inserting a finger inside, remove it and then slipped in two. My breath came short, I almost exploded. "Flattery will get you anywhere," I said against him, when he mounted me at last. I opened it for him, giving him easy access and he pushed himself inside, stopped and whispered "sorry" against my groan as he pushed a bit harder. There was the sound of a soft tearing in my ears and a welcome, full feeling and I knew it was done. It hurt when he moved, but his lovemaking did not last long and we climaxed together.

I thought I had wet myself and was shy when he pulled out, but he covered me, let me curl up in his arms and asked me if I felt okay and if he had hurt me terribly. I smiled against his arm and asked if we could do it again, soon?

"Okay, that's them," Charl says unexpectedly next to me. "Sit tight, okay?" he says before he gets out, slamming the door and locking it. A one-way glass partition is between the back of the van and the front, I hear him opening the sliding door. The magnificent, white beauty of a yacht has glided in without me noticing. It just floats there on the calm rhythm of the waves, as if it materialized by magic.

A jovial, quite stout gentleman makes an appearance around the back of the SUV, I see him in the rearview mirror. He is biting on a cigar, its tip glows red and he exhales clouds of smoke without taking it out of his mouth. He is dressed in a shirt with a Mayan theme and three-quarter slacks threatening to slip down under the weight of his stomach resting on the waistband.

"Ah! Pretty little birds you lot have!" he speaks to Charl, busy loading the crates on a trolley.

"We sure do, Mister Khan!" Charl answers him.

"You lucky devil, you!" He has a cruel laugh. "Filthy old bastard!" I think, without reason.

The rest of the transaction happens at the back of

the SUV; I see Charl returning, reflected in the side view mirror, with a suitcase. He unlocks and starts the engine without saying a word.

Something my mother said jumps to my mind. "Nasty business, my sweet. But the nastiness pays well. So, we ignore it for what it is." Strange, I cannot help thinking as we leave the harbor area, she never said 'for what it is.' Contempt maybe? Most probably!

CHAPTER 3

My heart is broken. Jean is leaving because she has got herself pregnant. It is only a few more months before we finish school. We had plans for the December holiday season before she was to leave to go and study a course in the medical field. Her parents are sending her away; the embarrassment proves too much for them because she is their only daughter, their girl who they are fiercely proud of and who would bring a degree of prestige to their family. It feels worse for me because I knew it would happen and I could not tell her. I tried to warn her and I know she was listening, but she was not hearing...

"It can still be made to be oraait, Jean!" I tried, but we did not have time because she had phoned me while her parents were out. They forbade her to be friends with me anymore. What did I do? It is a question I know the answer to because it is nothing I did, it is the nametag I am branded with. It became the cause of every death...

Of course, Benjamin stayed to finish his school year. He got away with "I don't sperm bastards!" and with it, also became a kind of hero to many of the younger boys. That is the way it is. I blame Jean's father who did not want any more scandal by avoiding a paternity test. Where is the justice in that? Add to that what Jean told me; it was not consensual. "I wanted him to stop! I told him, but he just was not listening..." I will hear those words for ever.

In the meanwhile, things at our house go their way, as it always does. I noticed a few new women, some mere girls like me and one who took a fancy to my father. Petunia. By the looks of it, it is mutual.

Naturally, my skills are developing too, and I feel proud of a personal achievement; a young guy got so out of breath with me, he swore my sex to be toxic. I took it as a compliment, of course! Besides, he was back for more of the same a week later...

It is in between all our daily comings and goings that I find my mother in her bed. It is a beautiful day outside. The sun is shining and a few clouds drift like lost thoughts in the sky. Her looks scare me.

"Mom," I whisper, slowly opening the door which stood a bit open. The curtains hang limp with the window open. From outside come faint sounds of conversation and the crashing of the waves.

"Hello, Sweet," she says but her tone of voice is animated and forced.

"Don't look so worried," Ludwick's voice comes from a chair next to her bed, I did not see him there at first glance.

"Can't you leave her alone?" I snap at him. I do not like his arrogance, never have.

I see my mother giving him a look, a communication without words. "I'll let you be, then," he grumbles as he gets up, leaving the newspaper he was reading on the chair. I take his seat without removing the newspaper, taking some satisfaction in sitting on his paper which he would certainly retrieve again.

"Mom?" We never had secrets and I feel left out because she certainly was not sick from yesterday! She is so pale and somehow "hollowed out" as if her body has no structure. I blame our busy lives. The money we made did not justify the time it stole from us.

"Sweet," she says, lying still. "It is more than just a cold, I am afraid." This was the excuse I was always given when I asked for my mother. I always accepted what they told me to be the truth.

"Daddy will take me for some tests soon, but I want you to continue with your life. Try not to worry."

This is more than I can handle, and my frustration shows in the deepening frown on my face. 'Mom, don't say that to me! It doesn't work that way! We don't hide things from each other!'"

"I'm sorry, Adelaide."

I realize that the news is not going to be good because she never, ever calls me anything but my pet name. "You are right. We do not have secrets. I have cancer, Sweet. Ovarian. My mother had it too, as did her mother. I have lived a long life compared to them, they all passed on in their thirties and here I am, nearing fifty-three!"

I do not know what to say, I sit there in my mother's room with the sunlight streaming in through the window, but my life's light is turned off. Its pitch dark in my corner.

CHAPTER 2

From the outside nothing has changed at The Bastion. There is still the house and the ocean and *Maria Madeline*, but she is not blooming anymore. It is winter and bitterly cold. Today the sky is cloudy and far out to sea a dark bank of clouds is gathering. The wind will bring it inland when it is ready, where it will pour out the pregnant clouds' burden.

I am outside. The garages are closed; there are no vehicles parked outside either. I am wearing my bathing costume under a tracksuit with my towel hung around my shoulders. I am keeping it from flying off by holding on to the ends which about reach the pockets on my hips. My flip-flops hit the white sand; it is surprisingly warm when I take my flip-flops off, although the surface feels cold. I should not be out. I should not go swimming. I know.

There is something missing at The Bastion. An integral part; its heart. My mother's place is empty. It does not matter where I look, I cannot find her and the sole place where I sense her presence is in the water. She went home quietly, her suffering mercifully at an end after only three months. She refused chemo and radiation and when the pain got too much. my father gave her morphine.

Her essence is with me here, with every stroke, plunging under every wave, with every surfacing and with every dive. Far up above, as I float, spent, the

21

seagulls swerve on their mysterious ways and the coastline shrinks further away. I am a strong swimmer but tired out. I had better turn around.

The welcome wave deposits me on the beach where the shock of the frigid wind is worse than realizing my towel has blown away. I hastily force my wet, sand-covered body into my tracksuit top which I rescued from a sandy grave.

I barely feel the sting of the sand against my face, as it blows with more force. A few pieces of debris cartwheel past me in a flash and disappear from my view. It is a steep incline to the back door. I skipped it so easily just a while ago but now it looks like a mountain. Our back door is not locked. I hear the phone ringing just as I step into the safety of The Bastion.

"Hello?" I answer the phone on what must be the last ring.

"Love? Where were you?" my father asks.

"Sorry, Dad. I went for a swim and just got back." There is silence on the other end.

"Puppet, it's not safe in this weather," he says, in the same tone he would use when telling me it is a sunny day out. I do not answer him. He knows why I went swimming - the same reason he is with Petunia now instead of at home. "Call me, anytime. I mean it. Bye now," he stammers before ending the call.

As a sign of respect for my mother, The Bastion's business is closed for a month. I do not want to be around my father who acts like a sleepwalker or a zombie most of the time.

He overdosed on sleeping tablets and was out of

sight for days. When he stumbled back to life, I just could not manage his and my own grief. He would burst out crying and not eat or respond to me, in any way. I had to shake him by his shoulders and scream "Stop it!"

It was me who phoned Clara Sims. Twenty-three, blonde, brown eyes and from Cape Town. Also known as Petunia. I got her number from my father's filing cabinet, which stood unlocked as he left it when I cried out to him, "She is gone, Daddy! Help!" My mother died in their room, in their bed, surrounded by her legacy. Petunia came by and to my utter relief, he, willingly, went with her.

"Get yourself a pet, Honey," was Jewel's advice to me. She oversees the 'powders, brushes and any others', as it was commonly known. Jewel did all the girls' make-up, hair, and waxing (men too!) before their sessions. She is a professional who landed on tough times when the film company she worked for went bankrupt. We were lucky she answered our advertisement and could start immediately.

Jewel is blond with a quirky sense of humor. She once told me about a child, if it was hers she did not say, and I did not ask. We are close and we like similar things.

The shower I took revived me, I sit staring out my bedroom window at the storm raging, letting my thoughts run free like the wild horses of Neptune over the breakers. I masturbate as my mother told me to; I am lazily calm and restful.

Charl and Jimmy were my mother's private film men. They were seriously just as shaken as us when they heard about my mother's passing. Typically men, they gave me bear hugs and grumbled: "Good luck, see ya soon, okay?"

The men my parents hired all had some specialty other than the work they did for us. They were all physically fit and worked out at the gymnasium, military type guys who could use guns, track people and I suspect, kill them too. Gregory, Ursula and Biddy make up the batch of "shooters" or filmmakers. I received a lovely bunch of flowers from them and a short film they compiled with some of my mother's sessions. Even they knew a lot about self-defense, first aid and I pleaded with them all to come back after the unexpected vacation. They all came from surrounding areas and have been working for us for many years. It was my duty to ask for their return. I stepped into the shoes of taking responsibility for my legacy quite naturally.

I smile a sad smile at my mother in her rock overlooking the ocean; the pointed rock can be seen from all the rooms. Her memorial service was held in East London (we could never have dared to bury her from the local church) and my dad and I brought back her ashes. We put her there, in a specially made alcove and sealed it. The simple words "Our Lilly, born 27 August 1931, left 18 April 1984" marks the stone. She was only fifty-three.

After the private moment, we went to scrub our border wall till our fingers and hands bled, through half of the night, to remove the spray-painted words: "A whore died here!" Charl and Jimmy would do it, but we wanted to. My dad and I sat against the wall afterwards looking up at the stars. "The brightest one must be her" he said, but I disagreed.

"Mom would not have wanted to stand out like that, but she sure is one of the most beautiful." He smiled at that.

"Sweet, you know she is the love of my life, right?" I did. I never thought otherwise.

Ludwick was booked into a "Trauma Recuperation Facility" which offered "intensive loss therapy" and was not in our way. Mercifully.

(Image from Pinterest)

CHAPTER 5

She is wearing heels, dressed in a pretty, noticeably short, black cocktail evening dress. She has brown eyes and pretty, kissable full lips. Hannah. She is as tall as I, a blonde with shoulder length hair tucked behind her ears. Jewel's work is perfect; it is just enough to look natural.

She steps out of her dress easily; her breasts are not confined in a bra; her nipples are erect. Jimmy and Biddy start filming, I am on the bed, waiting for her. I am nervous and I was told that it is okay because it was not acted out; our buyers liked it a lot.

Hannah reaches the bed and sits close to me. I have never been with a girl and I am not sure what to do. Hannah and I met briefly before the session and she assured me all I had to do was to relax and enjoy it.

"You're so beautiful," she whispers as she lies down next to me. "Can I touch you?" she asks and I nod.

I am in some prime lingerie, a brassiere and a thong. She softly lets her hand glide down my stomach, then lower until she touches me. She barely strokes, it is just a sensation. She retracts her hand, cups my chin, smiles and asks if she can have a kiss.

She kisses me for a long time, first without using her tongue and I am getting turned on in a way I have never imagined possible. My mother wanted to introduce me to "girl on girl action" before she got sick. My father is his old self again and full of fervor and ideas, I finally let him convince me; I have never seen my mother with another woman, but I know she indulged in it sometimes. "Men have such hard, muscular bodies," she had said, "it's so much different with a woman who knows exactly where to go besides right down, and softly!"

I longed for her as I forgot my shyness and let my tongue roam her mouth. She moaned softly, not asking my permission before she lets her hand slip into my thong.

Hannah keeps her hand there, stroking me but moves her kisses to my nipples, still in my brassiere. It expertly comes undone; her hand movements are quick and practiced. Her hand is fondling me again. She opens my lips softly. I open willingly, I am so wet. She stops suckling my nipples and kneels in between my legs, stripping me naked in a nanosecond. She opens my legs wider and smiles before she lets her head down there, caressing me with her tongue. I have always been spontaneous.

I held on to her head, whispering, "Don't stop, please," while she licks and sucks me to a shuddering orgasm; her tongue caressing a part of me undiscovered. I taste myself on her breath when she hoists herself up, kissing me again, her arms on both sides of me. She was not done.

I hear Jimmy and Biddy in the background, they are setting up another film roll. Biddy zooms in close the next minute, but she is only a shadow. My hands move down Hannah's body of their own accord. I want to please her as she pleases me. I want to see her naked. I want to taste her too. Her bum is tight and round, I cup it, kissing her. Her panty is a distraction, I want it off. I cup my hand with more intensity until I find the waistband and pull it down. Hannah laughs a naughty laugh, pulls herself up and strips. Her lips are fuller than mine and my spontaneity soars.

"Can I touch you?" I ask before she comes down on me. Hannah smiles and straddles me; I reach between her legs. She is as wet as I. She groans as I mimic her movements and apply strokes I know to be pleasing when I masturbate. It does not take long for her to come over my hand, I feel the involuntary traction of the muscles just beneath her skin on her inner legs, so that she shudders. She lets out a gasp when it is over.

There is a smile on her face when she kisses me, whispering in my ear, "You want more?"

CHAPTER 10

"It's been a long time since we have updated any of our equipment, Tracy. We have patched up 'cams and 'vids, I've seen some cool lightening stuff too." Biddy is in her element as we sit around my father's conference table adjacent to the bedroom he and my mother shared.

"Okay, Biddy, get a quote for the stuff we need. Make it extensive, we can filter before we make any decisions."

I knew we could afford whatever they wanted to be done. I could buy whatever I wanted. Money was no problem at all. Hell, I could have diamonds on the soles of my shoes if I wanted!

"Yajeel!" Biddy lets loose. I have no idea when last a meeting like this one was held. It must have been many years ago. It was triggered by a sudden drop in our film orders and my father was concerned. Being who he is, he asked outright what the reason was.

"Victor, it's not personal, Chum," Mister Khan said. "It's just that some of the other blokes' quality with regards to sound and zoom shots are a tad better, you know?" It remained a competitive industry; we had to do something and quickly. I had to; it was my business now.

We sit for a few more hours until I've heard Gregory's inserts. He handles both the editing and filming, along with Charl and Jimmy, who return with huge grins. I was so happy to see them!

"A friend of mine told me about 'mics for the ladies, set in earrings no bigger than a ten cent coin. It will definitely reduce background noise," Jimmy is saying.

"Ursula," I call our quietest member. Ursula is in her thirties, with bad skin but a sweet temper. She also dressed very smartly, and this gave me the idea. "Let's go through the rooms, I need some help. Our settings are out-of-date."

Ursula beams at me, showing an excitement I have not noticed before. "For sure!" she says, "give me a few minutes though, I have something on paper that might help!"

While I am waiting for her, my father appears, a frown on his forehead, not unlike mine! He is still a bit bleak around the gills and I do not think he is eating as he should but other than that, the dad I know - busy, awake and working, is back.

"Oh, sorry, Love," he says, almost walking into me. "Can I see you a sec?" He has limited time for the business' administration. Being a medical doctor on call leaves him with unpredictable work timetables in the busy hospitals of East London. Today is a rare day off for him.

I close the door from which we exited a while ago. "It's the advertisements," he says, sitting down at the head of the conference table, where his work papers are scattered. I see the filing cabinet is securely locked again, as it should be!

"What about them, Daddy?"

I know what our advertisements look like; I have

seen them often enough.

"Male housekeeper, slender, hardworking and willing is needed. Additional exceptional skills a deciding factor. Short term, please call..." or "Specialized female butler needed. Your own uniform, slender and with medical skills needed. Medium term, please call..." In later years we printed it with a spelling mistake on purpose, and we always received the reaction we needed. The interviews were left in the hands of our team as they made the films. They have always been given this privilege.

"What's wrong with them, Dad?" I ask.

"Honey, I'm concerned that we may find ourselves with a rat in our works."

I sat down opposite him. It is against the law to openly advertise our services; that is the reason for our cleverly disguised advertisements. Many long years ago the advertisements were only published in X-rated magazines, but it slowly changed and could now be found in locally published newspapers.

People in our industry know how to recognize them, but it also brought the risk of others finding out. It is the sole purpose of advertisements! The entire Gonubie and surrounding area know what we do, but they cannot prove it because of a system of legal eagles in prominent positions who are protecting us.

Our publishers are trusted individuals who are being paid by the business. "Daddy, what happened?"

He is silent for a while before he looks directly at me. "I have been thinking it must be one of our publishers. A lady answered an advert, but Charl realized that there was someone else on the same line. The SAPD. He reacted quickly by simply saying the position was withdrawn. On another instance a couple came knocking, asking about our services. We never take couples. It is highly suspicious.

Two more similar incidents followed before Charl approached me. We decided to be more alert and determine if we could see a pattern and the reason. We did not breathe a word to you. Yesterday Charl recognized the lady who called earlier, attempting to mask her voice. That is when I started thinking. They are amateurs, the rat must be a tame one, not a publisher. One that knows our layout.

"Who would want to harm us?" my father asks, shrugging. "Just a whole village and then some more!" he answered his own question, he does not give me time to say a word "But do not worry, Love, we can play cat. A big, old, nasty cat."

Ursula tentatively coughs before knocking. I smile at my father, wondering who would want to harm me? Just a whole village, Benjamin, Jean's or even Jacques' parents and then some more.

CHAPTER 11

Hannah and I have been together many times over the last few months, and I have grown accustomed to her husky voice and often surprising ways of making love. We have just finished a session. The demand for us has grown and on the surface, everything was back on track.

The new lighting fixtures and our exclusively designed microphone earring pieces have arrived and two new cameras rolled noiselessly. Ursula had the rooms planned out masterfully; with a few pillows, throws, paintings, coffee tables and plant swops, it looked completely different. It was no small feat to achieve different effects for five rooms... excluding mine.

Petunia has moved in. I was a little unsettled thinking she would lie where my mother did, but my father was sensitive enough to redo their bedroom and bought a new bed. Somehow it made it a bit more acceptable. There was no talk of "love" and they had no plans to marry. It was only a matter of convenience. A wave they rode till it crashed.

I am mildly uncomfortable. There is a boat far out to sea; it has been lying there for a few days. From what I can see it is a pleasure boat; one which cost plenty of money. The sunlight ricochets off the ocean, catches the aerials and satellite dishes it carries on its deck and blindingly sends it right back into our rooms, like a prying eye. Ursula had blinds installed which helped with the picture clarity but even through it, flashes of the offending thing shone through.

The other reason for my discomfort is Ludwick. His convertible materialized like a bird of doom one sunny afternoon. My father had the *Maria Madeline* replaced by a simple evergreen creeper with leaves as large as a grown man's hand. I was saying my goodbyes to Hannah under it when I noticed the car on the periphery of my vision. Our friendship grew strong and I relied on it; who else could I talk "women stuff" to? She was also an excellent tutor...

Ludwick is in my father's office. I can hear the rise and fall of conversation. It sounds more like an intense argument. I decide to hang around for a while; of course, I have every right to enter the office unannounced, but I still have the common courtesy to wait. "Think about it, my friend!" I hear Ludwick's voice clearer as if he is nearing the door. "That's all I'm asking." The next minute he is right in the door, on his way out. I have just enough time to dive into the bedroom, luckily without Petunia in attendance. I can hear clearly what is being said.

"Ludwick, you were a paying guest, I respect that. But you know very well that The Bastion is run by set rules. That is why we are still in business after all this time. You go and count those who folded and the reasons why!"

I see Ludwick leaving, in a dark temper judging by his red face. It is probably because my father used the past tense... Well, I am glad that my father also does not like him much!

"Dad?" I say. He lifts his head and beckons me in. "You heard; I suppose?" he says, but he is not angry anymore.

"Well," is all he says when I sit down. "Poppet, can we talk about it tonight? He is suggesting changes, 'as a friend' and I do not blatantly want to shoot it down. He just caught me at a tough time. I'm booked for theatre."

"Yes, sure Dad," I reassure him, getting up as he is making ready to leave. "Can we also talk about the prying eye?" I ask.

He nods, knowing what I refer to, leading me with his hand in the small of my back to the door.

"It's getting on my nerves too."

I decide to cook for the two, no, three of us tonight. We have a cook who leaves us meals in the freezer and refrigerator, but I think I will give him a well deserved break.

It is an hour after my father left and The Bastion is pleasantly quiet.

"Hallo!" Petunia says behind my back. I am still surprised to find her in the house although she is silent enough in her comings and goings. She is also booked for sessions and I recall seeing her with Jewel earlier this morning.

I am searching my mind for some mutual subject for conversation. "Hi, there!" I speak. She is so young! I recognize with a shock; I would even say a year or two younger than me. She is pretty. Her long hair is in a ponytail, there is a red tint in the darkness where the sun shines on it. She is standing by the sink with her back to the window, smiling shyly. I have never thought about it, how uncomfortable the situation must surely make her feel.

"Can I help?" she asks, "I love cooking, if you're about to cook? There's so little time for it, don't you think?"

Petunia is pleasant to talk to, she has no airs and graces and before long we chat companionably while we chop, stir and cook until the kitchen fills with enticing aromas. We talk mostly about music, film stars and when we get to the subject of school, she falls silent. I have one more subject to write for my final exams to be over. Petunia had dropped out for reasons which were not my concern.

When my father arrives, much later than usual, he is tired and visibly worn out. He brightens when he sees the carefully set table and home-cooked meal. We have a wonderful time, with the soothing sound of waves gently rolling onto the beach in the background.

I cannot deny it; it started to become weird when Petunia and my father kissed, it was brief, just a friendly token of gratitude but I excused myself hastily and it worried me. Age has never bothered me before; both my parents and I have had encounters with partners both older and younger.

Back in my own room, I lie on my bed in the light of the full moon. It is there, the boat. There are lights on and I feel strangely exposed. The soft knock of my father comes just at the right time because I feel ready to scream at it to go away; for it to leave us alone.

CHAPTER 12

My father turns on the radio in his office. He loves Enya's music and her music can always be heard in The Bastion. There is nothing unusual about it besides the fact that it is a little too loud. He closes the door and whispers in my ear, "Sit down, Honey. I'll explain."

He sits close to me so that we can hear one another. The office lights are turned down low too, the atmosphere feels stifled and foreboding.

"The prying eye," he says, "all those fancy satellite dishes are zoomed in on The Bastion."

I feel goosebumps on my skin, we have never been pursued in such a way. What we did could never be proven by any accuser over many years!

"Charl has military intelligence training; he is able to start digging until we get to the truth. For now, we don't have much to go on. She belongs to Frank Crombie, an oil magnate. His boat, *Illinois* and her crew has permission for docking for conducting 'deep ocean oil excavation research.' We believe there is more to it. She is not doing anything illegal except interfering in our privacy and it could easily be explained away - crossed signals, sound wave inconsistency or simply just by mistake. For now, we are taking preventative measures. Charl and the guys are going to install a temporary speaker system throughout, it will cause just enough of a disturbance to interfere with their signals, and we keep our blinds shut."

I get up to pour us each a whiskey and soda; my father keeps a bottle in his top drawer. I have been introduced to alcohol and enjoyed a tot on occasion.

"Dad, does it mean we were wrong in our assumptions of the advertisers being involved?"

He nods, swirling his drink in his glass. "I think so, Honey. Whoever is behind this wants access; the phone calls prove that. It must have a connection with *Illinois*, of that I am certain. What remains a question is why? And we can't dismiss the villagers yet." He smiles and lets his hand run through my hair; a mannerism he has liked since I was a child. "I'm proud of you," he says. "How I wish Mom could still be here. I miss her, you know that, hey Poppet?"

I set my glass down on the glass tabletop. "Thank you, Dad, I know. I miss her too."

A stray beam of what looks like a searchlight makes a desperate attempt to penetrate the blinds. Its broken beam shatters shards of weird patterns on the wall.

"Are we safe, Dad?" I ask, more than a little frightened all of a sudden.

"Sure, Honey," he says. "I'll kill the dragon for my family, remember? Guards were arranged; they assumed stations around the house a few hours earlier. Please be careful when you go for a swim, even with the guards around? For me, please, Poppet!"

"Sure, Daddy," I promise him.

He yawns, "I'm bushed!" he says, lazily getting up.

"Daddy, we can talk about Ludwick another time..."

I falter, although I am burning to know what he has suggested.

My father hands me a file I had not noticed lying next to the stereo system. "It's all in here, Love," he says, turning the system off and putting his finger against his lips in the gesture used for "silence." I nod, kiss him goodnight and we leave his office together.

CHAPTER 13

I am not in a hurry to go to sleep; I have time. I open my blinds deliberately and switch on my bedside lamp.

It is there. It is not trying to hide. I want to be as bold as it. I want to defy it. It with its audacity to dare to terrify us. The windows are open and there is a very pleasant breeze blowing through the curtains. With it comes sound; that of the rolling waves and smell - salty, sweet and sad.

I put the file on my pillow and head for the shower. There is time enough to read later. I open the tap at full blast. The shower lets loose a powerful jet of warm water. My sadness has a smell. It will be different for everybody, I guess. Sad smells like coconut sunscreen, strawberry ice cream and Dettol disinfectant.

I recall when I was but a baby still and my parents brought me to the beach and the smell of the coconut sunscreen they used. When I was a little older, the strawberry ice cream we kept in the freezer and how my father used to struggle to scoop it out into round balls to stack on the cones. A few years later, the many Dettol baths my mother prepared for me when I was out in the sun too long and got burned to a fiery, very painful crimson which would peel off when the blisters got better. Why is it sad? Because it went by like a vague impression which passes before your eyes could focus on it properly.

I close the blinds before I got to reading, but only because I sleep naked. The document is typed and has very few typing errors, I noticed at first glance. There is no introductory paragraph or a "dear" person to introduce the body which follows. It is but a plain, numerically stipulated paper. On the second page is a lone paragraph, without a number, which I read first.

"There's a new tendency in the pornographic film industry. Reputed filmmakers must remain competitive in this market and continuously develop playful, entertaining and fresh material. The suggestions in this document are only ideas and are meant as inspiration, not criticism. Please allow me to boast that marketing as such, isn't completely out of my area of expertise." It is not signed.

1) "Outdoors – why should all the sexual encounters be in bed? I have had the privilege to screen a competitor's work (through mutual friends) who is experimenting in shooting sexual scenes outdoors. His material is slapdash, I will admit as much. There is a lot of unexplored possibilities here...

2) Mixed – surely in an enlightened age, people sleep with partners who are from a different skin color than their own? I feel it should be explored; it will be extremely exciting.

3) Close-ups – of the act. Why not get clear, specific shots of penetration and climax? It is not only facial expressions which tell a story!

4) Gays – It is surely a taboo subject, as much as lesbians are, but the latter proved very profitable. Why

not explore the other?

5)   Style-specific – Kama sutra... Marketing variety films but sell it in a style-specific category. Everybody knows about Kama Sutra, but I suspect only a very few have the guts to experiment!

6)   Threesomes – Now surely, I will not be convinced it never crossed anybody's mind..."

A light drizzle sifts down, the way it happens at the coast. I need not hear it; I can smell and feel it in the change of the breeze. It is just a tad cold and it does not have the strength to make the curtains move, the blinds are not solid enough to keep the wind out.

Ludwick is a botanist by profession. He is not in the least qualified or knowledgeable in our field but as hard as it is for me to admit; he has a healthy enough sexual appetite for his fifty-six years to think in an unorthodox way. This was the reason my mother fancied him. Not his personality but rather this? I wish I could ask her; I wish I had asked her many things.

I get up to close the window a bit, the raindrops plop musically on the leaves in the garden and a choir of frogs start up. That is when I notice the ocean. It is as it should be. The cancerous growth is gone, or has it only shut its eye?

CHAPTER 14

"Hannah? I cannot hear you, is something wrong?"

We had a session booked and a meeting scheduled to assess the general feeling of some proposed changes. I also invited Ludwick, on my father's recommendation, as it was his brainchild.

Hannah has phoned me on our landline. I took her call in private on one of the mobile phones. I can hear her faintly through the unbelievably bad connection, I have no idea where she is phoning from. It sounds alarming as if she is struggling to breathe.

I speak louder, even a little frantic. "Hannah! Hannah? What is wrong?" There are a few seconds' silence, I am not sure if we are disconnected but then I hear her voice, it sounds raspy and sore.

"Something's wrong, Tracy. I do not know what it is, I need help. Please."

I am in overdrive in a second. "Where are you?" I scribble down her address in East London; at least a thirty-minute drive. "I'm on my way, Hannah."

"Biddy, I'll be back" I manage calmly. "My father will be back from his consultation soon, please tell him to stay home. It's an emergency."

Biddy nods. "Will do," she says, not flustered in the least.

I storm down the staircase. I am using my mother's car, it is closest and I do not have to reverse as far. I am still learning to drive and only have my learners' license. I am not supposed to drive alone but I am high on adrenaline and I may act a bit irresponsibly, I register in the back of my mind.

It is almost ten and the traffic should have quieted down as most people will be at work already. I leave Gonubie in a dust cloud, grinding the gears. I feel foolish, but Hannah needs my help. My mother's feisty car climbs onto the highway and I start to feel more confident behind the wheel, taking care not to drive too fast and alert the traffic police. It is the last thing I need!

The kilometers flash by uneventfully. It is a warm day; the ocean lies like a sleeping reptile on the horizon - cool and in stark contrast to the heat that surrounds it. I think about my mother and switch on the radio but there is only static so I turn it off.

I can see East London approaching and slow down. There are more heavy trucks arriving and departing from the harbor, the lanes are narrow and I must be careful. I am also not certain how far the turn-off on the N16 to the Port Elizabeth slipway is. I keep to my left and stay behind a truck carrying timber, then notice the slipway.

Hannah lives in Lauderdale, one of the older suburbs and not entirely alien to me. I remember there used to be a supermarket where we went shopping. In those years it was about the best and nearest. The timber - carrying truck turns off and I miss the comforting bulk, but I need not worry, on the next corner is a traffic light and it is red. This will give me time to read the street names.

To my left are industrial buildings so I concentrate on my right. The sun shines mercilessly down, blinding on the smooth surfaces of car windows, shop's windows, car bonnets and roofs. *Bougainvillea* are blooming in eye-catching purples, pinks and whites all along the road. The lawns are particularly green and lush, we had a good rainy season. The traffic light changes and I stay in the right lane, ignoring the obviously irritated driver behind me. I see him irritably drumming his fingers on the steering wheel. Collard Street, I see on a name board, the turnoff is about three meters away. I switch on the indicator. I just need to find number fourteen. The sudden closing of the tops of the trees in the narrow street is claustrophobic and it is suddenly darker too, I take off my sunglasses.

Number twenty-two is on my left, the houses on my right do not have visible numbers. I am relieved that it is a quiet street; only the railway line is visible on a steep incline but there are no vehicles. I hit a nasty pothole which almost jerks the steering wheel from my grip and I sharpen my concentration. I slow down to number sixteen. There, across the street, is number fourteen. It is an old station house, as it was lovingly known. All the houses look the same, they were built for the families of the SARA employees (South-African Railway Association) and was classified as low-cost housing. Father time is cruel and neglect stepped in when SARA was privatized and the nifty station houses were sold for far less than they were worth.

I jump out and run up to the front door; Hannah's

house does not have a fence. She must have been waiting.

She opens the door just as I step onto the porch. I have never seen anybody so pale.

"Tracy" she whispers as I reach for her, "help me."

I hold her, "It's okay, I'm here."

CHAPTER 15

"She's better, Love," my dad reassures me. "Let her sleep, she is safe here with us. You did the right thing to bring her here."

It was a nightmare return trip; I was half dragging, half praying and half forcing Hannah back to the car. It did not help that she could not tell me if she was in any pain or discomfort. She felt too warm against me and even the few sips of water I gave her came right up. I was scared. When we were both in the car, I threw caution to the wind and made for home with haste.

Hannah was slumped in the passenger seat, asleep, but her breathing did not sound normal. I tried talking to her, but I had to concentrate extra hard on the road and the traffic around us which had multiplied in less than thirty minutes. I did manage to grab a hold of her hand, which she took and held all the way. I heard her whisper, "Thank you," but she had no strength left to say anything more.

My father came running to the gate when he saw the car and carried her inside in his arms. He spent a long time with her. He had me fetch his medical bag, the large one, and frowned his stern frown.

Now the worms crawl out of the woodwork; the ugly truth surfaces and it has to do with Hannah who is sitting up in her bed. We made her comfortable in a small rooftop room. It used to be my playroom - it is secluded and incredibly quiet. My mother had it refurbished a year before she passed away, but it was never used as an entertainment room. The rafters which hold the roof are sturdy; it is still the original yellowwood The Bastion was fitted with. If we put a ceiling in, it would be covered. As it is, the film sound echoed horribly because of a combination of the elongated shape and the lack of a ceiling, so the room stayed pleasantly untouched. It has a beautiful square window overlooking the ocean. This reminds me of the unwelcome guest, the cancerous growth, the ever-present prying eye which has been harassing us for the past few days with its infrequent presentations. Just when we thought it was gone it would reappear. It was splendid in its absence now.

"You were being poisoned," my father is telling her, sitting in a rocking chair next to her bed. "You inhaled small amounts of poisonous, odorless gas fumes, at night when you were asleep. The last dosage was meant to kill you, but the oxygen concentration in your blood stayed sufficient to keep you alive. If you had stayed a night or two longer, we may have seen a different outcome."

Hannah is still very pale; she is lying with her head on my shoulder which feels comforting.

"I have a suspicion that you know more than you are telling," my father continues, in a coaxing voice. When she is quiet, he says, "Isn't that the reason why you didn't call an ambulance?" I will my father to stop what sounds like an accusation, I have started to feel a protectiveness towards Hannah grow inside of me.

She moves, sitting unaided but she is holding

onto my hand, before she speaks.

"I have loathed his arrogance since I was introduced to him. "The Crombie family are a well-to-do bunch' my mother said. We were at loggerheads about my unmarried status at the time," she explains. "I just could not drive the idea of a woman loving another in such a way, home to my mother. She would accuse me of being invaded by Satan. I was tired of the fighting.

"Mother wanted her freedom; she did not want to be chained down by a grown-up child. Things were difficult enough." Hannah lets go of my hand to rub her temples. She looks tired, but she smiles at me, a bit uncertainly. I know we must get through this before she, and we, can rest.

"I married Frank," she continues. "The 'gentleman' soon showed his true colors. 'Ba!' he would shout at me 'I married you because of your beauty! You have no brains, remember that!' After three years I just could not stand it anymore. I was careful not to fall pregnant because I was planning an escape from a life I never wanted. There was a friend, a girlfriend I started seeing and Frank found out. He was livid!

"He swore he would let me be circumcised. When Geraldine was murdered I knew for certain that I was not safe. Then the unimaginable thing happened - he let me go, or so I thought. I am sure he got bored and he knew he could find me, anywhere and at any time. I have hurt his ego and he wants revenge. If he could harm you in the process, he would.

"I am sorry. I am so sorry. *Illinois* is his, he bought

her as a pleasure boat and would disappear for days with it. I did not mind that. In the meantime, he most probably had it fitted with spyware. He must have been tracking me. He bargained on my death after he followed me here, all the while accumulating enough evidence about The Bastion..."

CHAPTER 15

He is a bit rough with me and I do not care about it much. His penis is larger than any I have seen and it is his obvious pride, but his lovemaking technique lacks tenderness. I decided to act it out, he would be spent sooner if I do. If only he would be a bit more careful with my nipples, he is hurting me! Today is one of the few days that I am not enjoying my session.

We are outside today, in a secluded spot of our garden. It is warm. The anti-glare screens Biddy put up concentrate the heat on us. I moan, for effect, but in truth I am turning my head a little to catch the lukewarm breeze from a lone fan put up just out of shot. I catch a glimpse of Jimmy zooming in on the area between my legs. I cannot help but award him with a naughty smile. He colors immediately. I am acutely aware of my woman power but at times am still surprised by it. Sex scenes are all our staff films, I wonder if they ever get bored with it.

At last, he is there and not a minute too soon. My mind is a million miles away.

"You okay, Hon'?" Jewel asks as I step into the welcome coolness of The Bastion with its white tiles and open plan lounge - and kitchen area. I am only wearing a light cotton see-through gown; I need a shower! Jewel is pouring juice from an iced container; they were as much a part of the household as my father and me.

"I'm okay, thanks Jewel," I smile. "I just did not like my partner much, he was a bit rough."

Her mood changes visibly. "Then he'll not be welcome here again. Xo poke," she says. "Mark his name."

Jewel is fiercely protective of me. All the applicants who are selected, sign the Jene Turaq and it gets filed in my father's office. The files marked with a black cross are applicants who need not waste their time again. It is also the only place where the applicant's personal details are mentioned. It contains a medical examination; we will never take any chance of catching STD's or any other illness. Only my father and now me, have access to it. Any member of our staff with a grievance, either communicated to them or observed, will print the name together with the broken rule or rules and give it to me or my father. We do not ask questions and we do not accept apologies.

I know Hannah had used her birth name; if she had not my father and Charl would have picked up the link between *Illinois'* owner and Hannah. That is not what is worrying me.

The shower is uplifting, I am ridding myself of my partner's sperm, dripping down my legs. My father inserted a "female condom" inside of both Hannah and me, protecting us from getting pregnant. It is his own design but not patented yet. We are together, she has moved in with me.

My father decided not to give me the hormone injections my mother also received because he suspected a link between it and ovarian cancer. I close the cold jet of water and step into my room. Hannah's clothes are still on the bedcover; she has been sharing my bed for a while. I dress quickly and make my way outside. This is the best time for slipping out because everybody is busy. My father was booked for a surgery and left early. He has been remarkably busier since Petunia left. Their time together ran out.

Hannah has a session booked in five minutes time and Ludwick is supervising. It is also a very sore point for me but one I am ignoring for the moment. With the greatest difficulty.

I heard voices late last night and something else, a sound taking shape in my subconscious mind as that of a saber being drawn from its sheath. The distinctive pitch of a metal object being drawn sharply from its home. What is it my father always says? "I'll kill the dragon for my family…"

The beach is quiet and the sand burns under my feet. The night guards were dismissed; that is what made the voices suspicious. We had infra-red detectors installed at strategic points along the perimeter of our isolated beach and up the banks to within a meter of our doors. They trigger an alarm which could not be disabled in any other way but with a code. Of course, I know that a certain zone of the beach is disabled for outdoor filming, it will only be activated again in twenty minutes.

I am wearing shorts, a bra top and a loose shirt, keeping my eyes open for *Illinois* or any footprints. The yacht has been missing since yesterday. It is the longest time she has been gone.

Nearing the sea, where the water touches the

sand, I find what I am looking for, a disturbance in the natural course of things. Voices would travel up to my bedroom window on still nights. Overlooking the scene is the rock where my mother is resting. I dig out a man's shoe in the wet sand where the toe showed. It is new. The tide is coming in, I am just in time.

On my way back up the slope, I catch a glimpse of some crabs, scurrying away from some central spot. I go closer, feeling the wrath of the sun on my head. There is a bloody object which the crabs are feeding on. A man's hand, lying with the palm upwards. The severance wound shows an exceptionally clean, quick execution. Surgically precise. I take the ring from the cold finger and hurry home with it. I have two minutes before I trigger the alarm. The wedding band is burning hot in my short's pocket. It has a large calligraphy "C" engraved on the dark moonstone surface. I let go of the shoe.

My father had killed a dragon for his family.

(*St. Jordi killing the Dragon by Simon Bisley*)

CHAPTER 13

"Love, I know it's upsetting you, please understand?"

I am highly dismayed, to the point of irrational anger. We have never fought. My parents and I have always understood each other, compromised and accepted what we could not change.

Ludwick insists upon a percentage of our film sales. There is no denying that we are doing better than before because of some of the suggestions he proposed. He has practically moved into The Bastion and seems hardly ever to be anywhere else! In fact, my father is proposing that he supervises for two weeks. My father must go to China. He must go to receive a reward for 'outstanding surgical achievements.' Of course, he must go! He deserves it; he is working so hard!

"Surely, I can manage, Daddy! Biddy, Gregory, Charl, and Jimmy are here, Jewel, Ursula too and Hannah... "

I knew I was losing the argument. The Bastion is my legacy but my father is still my legal guardian. I proved to be quite the child I still was, for I made my feelings towards Ludwick clear in front of him. It would have been less of an insult if I had spat in his face.

My father left; I know he threatened Ludwick in confidence. But the latter all but glows with his temporary significance. The first thing he did, was to book Hannah for a lingerie photoshoot series in East

London. It is an honor to be chosen as a model for *Great-Spot*; our house has had models before but not recently. I also cannot deprive her; I have no right and she is so excited. This meant Hannah left just a day after my father, with Charl in tow, of which I was glad. *Great-G-spot* photographers will meet them at the *Imposing Victorian Inn*, one of the most luxurious playgrounds of the extremely rich and infamous.

She promised to phone me. It left me, Biddy, Jewel, Gregory, and Jimmy to fend for ourselves. We have bookings to address but a filmmaker fewer in attendance. It was going to take careful planning to make it work.

It happens that I find myself confronted with Ludwick on the very eve of my first evening alone. Biddy, Jewel, Gregory, Ursula, and Jimmy have left with my personal assurance that they need not worry.

Ludwick has taken my father's parking in the garage and closed the door. I was certain he had left.

"You don't like me much, do you, Tracy?" he asks, drawing out my name. He is at the refrigerator, taking out milk. I decide to be assertive because he is a guest in my home, an uninvited, unwelcome and uncourteous bastard who thinks he has some claim on my business.

"You know, Ludwick, I don't. It was all right when my mother was still here but since then all you've been is pompous." I soften my tone; he is still my senior and despite my dislike I do not want to hurt him. "I just think you're overstaying your welcome."

He comes closer. I am standing at the sink where

I just put down an empty coffee mug. He is wearing tight-fitting jeans which do not suit him; he is too skinny. In it, his erection is perfectly outlined. I detest him but I cannot let him know it.

"Oh?" he snarls. "I've been a part of The Bastion since your mother was a girl. I don't think you want to make me an enemy."

Ludwick has brown eyes and greying hair which threatens to become bald on top. He is athletically built, and I know from experience that lean men are often much stronger physically than they appear. Even an older man.

I feel the back of his hand on my face, the painful sting. I never saw it coming. It has me on my back on the kitchen floor. He rips off an apron from the counter and ties my hands behind my back.

"Scream all you like!" He laughs, overly excited.

I will not give him that satisfaction. I wait to see if he is going to follow through with his bravado. He is. He has a hold on my legs, pinning them down.

"Get up!" he shouts. "You dirty, smelly, whore of a child, get up!" It is not as easy with my hands tied but I manage. My cheek is sore. I can still feel the outline of his hand where he slapped me.

"Up!" he shouts. "Go to your room!" He finds this very funny. He pushes me onto my bed on my back. He sees one of Hannah's thongs on the floor, picks it up and stuffs it in my mouth.

"Taste your girlfriend while I make you a woman!" he says.

Tears well up in my eyes, not because I am afraid but because I am helpless. He pulls down my jeans and my panty and rips my T-shirt open, exposing my breasts. I am in the habit of not wearing a bra. He unzips his jeans, letting his penis free. He is hard and hairy with a crooked shaft. I want to laugh at him, but I cannot. He opens my legs.

"Xo chatè" he breathes, "no force" while he enters me. "Xo prokè," he says as he slaps my breasts, "no abuse." He leans over me, thrusting his member in and out. "Xo qabra" he grins, "no threat. I know what your holy father did to that man! I know where the poor bastard's body lies rotting!" With miraculous willpower, he pulls out. I am dry. It is painful. He spits on his hand and turns me over, rubbing the spit over my vagina before forcing himself inside of me from the back, "Xo vowrè, no favors," he breaths harder, "but I'm showing you one!" He thrusts harder. "Xo micotè" he shouts, "no acting of fantasies but you are mine!" He pulls out again, grabs me by my hair and turns me over. All I can do is watch him, silently, with hate boiling over. He sits over me, rubbing his crooked penis between my breasts. "Xo shakrè; no disclosure," he mouths, "I don't need to, because everybody knows!"

He is off me quickly, standing beside the bed. He smells like urine and sweat and lust like an animal possessed. He throws me off the bed. "Suck!" he says, pulling Hannah's underwear from my mouth. I take him, thinking of biting him but he reads my thoughts and pulls my ears. "Xo commeta, no dominance, but you'll listen to me, Whore!" He is close to climaxing but my senses are stumped, I cannot think clearly.

He forces my face away with the palm of his hand

on my forehead.

"Bend over!" He says with difficulty.

I stand on my knees, with my hands behind my back I cannot support my body weight as he slams into my back passage. This time I scream without the constriction in my mouth. It excites him. "Xo telmè," he screams. "No sodomy but you're a bitch," cupping my hips, tearing into me. Climaxing. "Pratè xo paca," he says, spent. "Anonymous identities. Call me 'Master!"

He gets up. I stay as I am, lying down. He wipes his mouth. "Xo barenè," he says in an ugly voice. "No orgies. Now I will taste you as a dog tastes his bitch."

CHAPTER 12

I cannot tell how I got through the days following my rape. There was a pain. I took Dettol baths, wishing the hurt I felt was that of a sunburn. My breasts were bruised and sex was out of the question. I asked Biddy to please cancel my sessions, I used my previous partner as a scapegoat, saying I was tender and sore.

Jewel immediately insisted on seeing me. I did play the acting of my life, feigning lightheartedness. "You're like an old woman with a leaking bladder!" I joked, managing to laugh. "I'm fine! No, leave me alone! Don't you have work to do?"

Ludwick trots around my home like a cock amongst its hens; we avoid each other. He does not ask why I canceled my sessions but lined up a few couples we have used before. He wanted to make gay films desperately, but our team refused to film it. We silently waited for him to trespass our unanimous decision but he was as smooth as butter and did not step out of his boundaries.

Hannah phones as she has promised.

"It's amazing!" she says, giggling. "The men are falling over their feet. How I wish you could be here! I am so happy with the experience; you know they are a highly professional bunch. There is nothing tacky about their shoots and they are very respectful."

I miss her. I want to tell her what happened, but I

cannot. Not without revealing that her husband was murdered. By my father! She blissfully believes that he simply got bored and went away. It is a fable my father embroidered upon too, saying we should not worry. I know in my heart that he knows that I know the truth.

A contact informed him that *Illinois* is docked in the Bahamas. That is the story he was selling.

"Tracy, I don't want you to worry," Hannah says, "Charl is never far away. It is going to take a bit longer than was planned. Their new line of swimwear arrived early, and they asked me to model for them! Great! Isn't it? It is good money!"

Of course I'm excited for her. I may get my opportunity to go soon. "That's so great!" I tell her. "It's super Hannah, you have to tell me everything! I cannot wait to see you!" My bruises will look much better by the time she gets back. Will I be capable of hiding yet another secret from her? Is it fair?

I use the time to doddle around The Bastion. It is not happening as often as I wish for. I met Gloria on the stairs; she is one of our domestic workers and I cannot recall when last I saw her!

I am heading for the basement; a storeroom where the history of The Bastion is kept safe. The Bastion is an old building which has undergone numerous restorations but the part I am going to is the least visited or even thought of.

I descend the old stairs; they smell old but not rotten. It becomes remarkably colder as the stairs lead down. The ancient steps have been left bare, worn smooth by many years of wear.

"The entertainment had to be kept secret," my mother had told me. "In those years ladies would be beheaded if found out. That's why it had to be kept underground, literally."

I search for the light switch on the wall, it is quite dark. The everyday sounds of the houses' activities change and gets distorted here, downstairs, like when you go underwater. I imagine the dull sound of what must be a vacuum cleaner and above it, a shrill laugh. It sounds like Jewel. She has a new boyfriend who makes her laugh. I am happy for her.

The globe stutters to life; it is not very bright. I am in front of a big, heavy old wooden door. On the surface is an engraving of a rose in an upturned knight's helmet.

"It signifies the power of a woman over a man," my mother had explained it to me. I was just a little girl when she brought me here for the first time.

"One day, history will also be yours, Sweet," she had said.

I reach up on my toes to the top of the doorframe where I know the key is kept. I find it. It is an old, heavy, brass key.

I push the release clip just below the handle and the door swings open. The inside is a surprise because it is so different than one would imagine it to be. It is a light, airy room and not a dark, foreboding dungeon. There are no rats as big as poodles. Alas, both are modern inventions. The light source comes on via a clever door – triggered mechanism and the fresh air comes from a combination air conditioning and humidity control system. This is necessary to preserve the fragile paper records on the shelves. I will not deny that it is dusty under the lights, but that is to be expected! It does not smell old or new. I would say it smells ageless. Ageless smells like that of women of many generations past. Strong, formidable, extraordinarily rich women; of whom The Bastion was their legacy. I know this because five generations of their captured likenesses line the two opposite walls in gold-and diamond frames.

In the center of the room is a wooden table; an incredibly old, heavy writing table. If I go over there, I will find Jene Turaq on it. It is written in the original compiler's hand. The fragile, irreplaceable document is immortalized in a glass frame fastened on the table.

I come to rest on the chair at the writing table, imagining the women who penned those words. Proud ladies who kept their heritage safe to hand it over, with pride, to the next generation. I am from that generation. It is now my legacy. I can walk the streets with diamonds on the soles of my shoes, with pride. I will not do any less. I also will not allow Ludwick to walk away from what he did.

A calm settles over me. It feels like reassuring whispers from the women around me. Like protective arms. It gives me a power I did not fathom until this moment.

I open the old desk's drawer. In it is a pen and some paper sheaves. I print a name on it in capital letters. I list the entire Jene Turaq underneath and fold it. I place it on the stack on the shelf behind me. It belongs there with all the others who dared to disobey it. What makes these ones different from the ones upstairs in my father's cabinet, besides that it is ancient?

All the perpetrators whose names were in this room were killed for their discrepancies. That was the only and just punishment. It does not matter that it happened many yellow years ago.

CHAPTER 15

"Slowly," she moans.

I am ecstatic with joy; I am so relieved that Hannah is back. She looks well rested despite the grueling routine she told me all about. She brought me back some photos in an album. Goodness! She is so beautiful! I have two fingers inside of her, moving them rhythmically in and out. I am teasing her with my tongue with alternating pressure. I know I am driving her crazy. I am crazy with lust too. Her breathing tells me she is near. Will I let her climax? I smile. No. No, not yet.

I take my fingers out, but I keep my tongue there, licking her with feather-light strokes. Hannah arcs her back, begging me. Opening. Presenting herself. Oh yes. I will let her. In a minute. I open her legs wider with my arms, pressing my tongue inside of her as deep as I can. She has her hand on herself, stroking. Her anticipation piques. Her breathing comes faster. She moans deliciously while she thrusts with her lower body. Then she is there. Once. Twice... and once more.

We are alone. I want her for myself without the film crew present. It does not matter that we are in all probability making the elusive 'best film ever'. I crawl up onto her, seeking the warmth of her mouth, craving the feeling of her probing tongue.

"What have I done to deserve the special

treatment?" she asks, still out of breath.

"Oh!" I smile against her mouth, seeking it with my lips. "It's punishment," I answer while her hand moves to my nipples. I let out a soft moan as she cups my breast, "for going away." She kisses me hard, rolling me on my back. She always seeks out the ripples of the scar on my hip, she calls it hers.

We are in the rooftop room, away from the immediate world. She sits astride me, gently moving back and forth. I can just feel her on me. Then she smiles a crooked smile. I inhale with expectation. Hannah moves one leg between mine and pulls me up. We touch, there, down. She anchors herself with her arms behind her, I do the same. "Sit more on me," she whispers. I move up a bit and feel her wetness instantly. It takes all my self -control not to exclaim. I never use Gods' name like that.

"Do you like it?" she smiles into my eyes.

Hannah lunges, I move with her as the feeling of our friction increases. She has her head back, her breasts bobbing with the movement and our bodies clapping hands... body heat builds up between our legs. It smells sweet and wet. It is soft and hugging. I explode a second before her, forcing myself more on her at the last moment. She does not waste a minute holding my head, kissing me but it is without the eagerness, it is tender and loving.

Sunday is one of the most beautiful because everything is so utterly perfect, from the weather to this moment. My father has gone fishing, The Bastion is locked and secured. Hannah and I are our own masters.

My father and I have not spoken about the recent past at all. As if by mutual consent we decided that if we did not mention anything, nothing would happen. On surface value, the world is a lovely place.

After a swim yesterday, with my mother's essence close to me, I finally got the clarity I needed. I am spurred on by my ancestral heritage and my feelings for Hannah because I want her to be a permanent part of my life if she wishes. Xo chatè and xo vowrè. I cannot break the Jene Turaq, it is unthinkable but what if I do not need to? There is no record of how the previous ladies of the house got rid of the guilt. Now that would be telling...

I let Hannah snuggle in my arms, holding on to her tight. "Comme unto," I whisper in her hair.

"I don't know that one," she says, lifting her head.

"It's because it's so special," I say. "It means 'I'll love you, evermore.'" We will sleep now and who knows? Later. Much later we may do the same.

"Comme untè," Hannah sighs before sleep comes to claim us as his.

CHAPTER 20

I have finally managed to obtain my driver's license, a freedom newfound. I bought an Audi Quattro convertible in red with white leather seats and another one in black for my girlfriend. Simply because I can. I want to spoil her.

It is a scorching, muggy day in December. The opened rooftop does little to cool me; the wind is warm. Then again, my blood is boiling without the aid of the weather. I have never been one to sing along with the hits over the radio. I relish the silence more.

I am heading towards Elliot. Ludwick stays there, his address is in our cabinet. His file is one of the oldest; he has been a guest for over fifteen years. I also know he is an insulin dependant diabetic. I have two syringes in my handbag. With compliments from my father.

The road is quiet, I am heading inland. There is a dark coloration on the horizon where a thunderstorm is brewing. I may run into it. At least it will break the heatwave. It is green everywhere I look, dotted with the hardened whitethorn trees common to the area. It is mostly cattle farms and timber but there are two prominent poultry farms in the area as well. I let my thoughts run free like the running of the tires on the tar.

I am wearing one of my mother's dresses, it is a flowery dress that she never got to wear. It is dangerously short! I have high heeled open toe shoes on, my hair is loose. The green leave pattern on the dress accentuates my blue eyes. I have tied a scarf loosely around my head on impulse, feeling like a movie star! This combination together with the maroon-colored teardrop earrings is quite striking. That is the idea. I have squirted some Blue Gras perfume on my pulse, neck and between my breasts. It was my mother's favorite scent.

Elliot is a small town; it is at the foothills of the Drakensberg in the Eastern Cape Midlands. The farm I am heading to is called "Ooster Ster" (Eastern Star). It is partly a guest farm which also offers fly fishing, hiking trails and wildflower tours. It is more widely known for its exceptional botanical garden and the botanist behind it, Dr. Ludwick Lees.

It is a two-hundred-and-forty-three-kilometer drive to Elliot and another fifteen to the farm. I am not familiar with the area. It is breathtakingly beautiful with mountains and unexpected stretches of open fields.

I can see how easy it is for Ludwick to leave home for a few days without raising any suspicion. He has business in East London, at the University where he also cultivates rare and exotic species and teaches evening classes by invitation. He is retired.

My car hits the dirt road; I drive slower. Dirt roads are tricky. It may look smooth but the loose sandbanks on the sides can easily cause an accident if it is hit with speed. I have seen large trucks capsized by sandbanks.

I see the sandstone farmhouse on the hill. It is a picturesque old house; sturdy and strong. I drive through the open gates. Neat parking spaces are marked out on a paved area in front of the house. There are two other parked cars. In the garages to the right of the house, I glimpse Ludwick's car and a smaller, white car. I have never thought of him as a married man... I wonder if he has children. There is a *Maria Madeline* in full bloom near the front door. I cannot help but wonder if my father removed ours because it originated from here?

The front door is open. I can hear people talking. Somebody must have told a joke because suddenly he or she bursts out laughing. There is the tell-tale smell of a home cooked meal drifting to the door. Leg of lamb with rosemary, fried potatoes with garlic butter, butternut sprinkled with cinnamon sugar and something overly sweet. A Malva pudding.

I feel out of place, which I am. I want to turn around and leave but a big, sloppy-mouthed dog with kind brown eyes and a wagging tail notices me where it lies sleeping behind the back of a chair. I am such a sucker for dogs! I wonder, surprised, why I never got myself one.

"Hello boy!" I whisper, a trail of saliva lands on my dress as I kneel, but I could not care. He has huge paws with short nails and his coat is a shining silver; he must be groomed regularly. His collar tag reads 'Buddy.' He wags his tail but to my consternation starts to emit tiny excited little barks. I realize he is just a pup and I cannot escape unseen.

"Buddy!" a woman's voice comes nearer, her

sandals are making clicking sounds on the wooden floor. "Oh, you naughty boy!" she exclaims, seeing me getting up from my knees. "He just about ruined your dress!" she says, mortified. It must be Ludwick's wife. She is slim and short with shoulder-length grey hair. Her brown eyes are searching mine for recognition but find none.

"I'm so sorry to intrude!" I smile. "Please don't be angry with Buddy! He is absolutely adorable!" To my relief, she laughs,

"He is that! And he knows it very well!" I must steer the conversation in my direction otherwise all would be lost. Ludwick must have heard my voice; he looks positively ashen as he comes closer, a little uncertain.

"Miss Lees?" I offer my hand, "I'm Annabelle. I should have called!" I see Ludwick hesitate behind his wife's back. "There he is! I am looking for Doctor!" I see Buddy hide behind his human mother as if his master's presence scares him.

I need to continue this pattern; it is sure to succeed. "Doctor!"

He comes from behind his wife.

"I just took a chance," I babble. "It is about the plant I showed you; it is not a white flower after all! Could it be a rare species of the same family? It is in town, you just must see it! The flower will wilt quickly, that is why I came impulsively." Where I am getting the words from is a mystery to me.

Miss Lees calls for Buddy. "Pleased to meet you!" She waves. "I will leave you two to it!"

I was correct in assuming his students and members of the public arrive here willy-nilly. I suppose guests looking for accommodation as well. I walk ahead, I hear him following.

"What the hell are you doing here?" he growls, every vestige of a human being gone. All I see is the animal smelling of urine, sweat, lust, sperm and blood. Mine. Where he forced himself inside of me.

CHAPTER 21

I lay it on, heavily.

"Ludwick, we can't ignore what happened. You may, but I can't." I raise my voice deliberately.

"Okay, okay," he says, panicky. "Not here! And not today!"

I smile my most provocative smile, letting my tongue play slowly over my lips. "Oh, but you're wrong. About it not being today."

We walk slowly in the direction of my car. I can hear children's voices now too.

"Your grandchildren?" I ask him,

"Yes," he answers. "I have three, my daughter is pregnant with the fourth. It will be the first boy." The second of kindness passes.

"Go away!" he says, under his breath.

"Oh, but I can't," I answer, "Not before we go for a little ride." I know I have him. His eyes are roaming over my body, his eyes are playing on my cleavage and running up my legs. He is not even wondering what it is about. He assumes it is for an enjoyable time. I also know he picked up the perfume I am wearing. It is bound to bring back memories.

"Connie!" he calls a blonde girl when she appeared outside with Buddy, throwing a tennis ball for the dog to fetch. She cannot throw it very far, but Buddy is making quite a show of running after it, missing it, and running back before he picks it up and drops the ball at her feet. He waits patiently for her to throw it again.

"Tell grand Mammie I'm just going to look at a plant. I will be back before lunch!"

The little girl nods. "Okay, Grandpop!"

He opens my car door, "I'll meet you at the *Horse and Hound Pub*. You cannot miss it."

Things are going far better than I had expected. I wait for his car, making certain he is following me. He does not want me to drop him at home again; a fact I was relying on because then he would have to explain. I open the clip of my handbag and feel inside it with my hand. The syringes are lying at the bottom on a handkerchief. There is nothing else inside.

I let the roof up, the sun is blinding and burning down vigorously. The dirt road is dry and the dust of our vehicles forms a tunnel behind us, like a snake stalking. I am glad when we get back on the tar road. I avoid looking in my rear-view mirror; I need not store an image of it in my mind.

There is an expectation there. Lust for something that never belonged to him. He is worse than an animal. I find a shady spot right in front of the pub. There are a few cars outside. Judging from the number plates, they must be tourists.

"That spot is mine," he says darkly as I lock my car. I bite my tongue.

"Aw, come on! You are a big boy! I am sure you can spare it for a lady for a few minutes!" I do not give him time to answer and walk into the cool of the pub. We take a booth near the window overlooking our cars.

"So, what do you want?" he asks as soon as he sits down.

"A cider would be nice, thank you," I answer sweetly, knowing it is not what he meant.

It is a spacious pub; it also offers pub lunch specials. The group of visitors are noisily clinking their beers; it is a men-only congregation.

"Two apple ciders," Ludwick tells the bartender who comes around to our table.

"Well, if it isn't the good doctor!" he beams. I am as relieved as Ludwick when the tinkle of a bell announces a food order is ready. The bartender chuckles and hops away, it looks as if he is doubling as a server.

I cross my legs on the small seat, giving Ludwick a glimpse of my white panty. He has the decency to blush when I watch him. Our ciders arrive, without glasses but I am in no mood to prolong this game any longer than I need to and refrain from asking for a glass. I take a sip, enjoying the bitter-sweet taste in my mouth which threatens to turn into gall when I see his self-satisfied grin. No more.

"So," I drawl, leaning forward on the table, showing him my breasts. He is excited, I notice his Adam's apple as he swallows. "What kind of dog is Buddy?" I could have hit him with a bucket of ice-cold water.

"Buddy? He's a... a..." he repeats, incredulous. "He's a Shar Pei. A rare breed."

I make a mental note of this because I really want one just like him. "How long have you been married?" I ask.

Ludwick is drinking his cider in big gulps. He decides to play the game, like a predator watching his kill.

"Francis and I have been married for forty-one years. We have three children, two sons, and a daughter."

I watch him, waiting. He orders another cider by showing the bartender the empty bottle.

"You don't even feel guilty about all the years you've been cheating her?"

He laughs, genuinely intrigued. "No! Why would I? You're going to ask me if I loved your mother," he says, now visibly a little unsteady. "Well, I did." His second cider arrives, without comment this time. "At first. But I wanted The Bastion more. Do I shock you? I feel nothing for your so-called legacy. Under my management, it could soar to heights unimaginable. I have proved it!"

I keep quiet, slowly sipping on my first cider. I do not care what he has to say. "No. You cannot shock me," I answer. "I'm beyond the point for you to shock me. You are disgusting."

Ludwick shifts on his seat and moves his face close to me. "Really? What if I told you I like fucking Buddy when everybody is asleep? I take him down to the cellar, where his howls can't be heard." He finally managed to sicken me.

"You sick, sick man," I say, getting up. He gets up too, drowning the last dregs of his cider. "On my tab, Brendan," he shouts. I do not wait for him but walk straight to his car. I am counting on it that he would be in a hurry to leave since the trip was obviously a waste of his time and I want him to believe that I pose no threat. I have the first syringe ready in my hand. He trips over his feet but manages to stay upright. He opens the door and gets in, winding down the window. The combination of the alcohol in his system and the searing of the sun makes him drip with sweat. He looks like the loathful thing he is.

I react as quickly as a snake which strikes. The needle lands in his upper arm. I inject the insulin. Ludwick's reactions are slow and disorientated. The second needle lands close to the first. Another injection of insulin.

"What the ...!" he stutters.

I am calm because I know there is nowhere for him to go for help. He does not even know what I injected him with.

"You'd better make for home," I say. "Here, take this," I say, handing him the handkerchief on which the syringes rested. I have placed the empty vials in my handbag. The handkerchief is one of his he has left at The Bastion. In it is the ring with the engraved 'C.'

He irritably throws it on the passenger seat without seeing the ring. I walk away.

Ludwick's wife's birth name is Crombie. Years ago when he still called himself Zachery, he had a passionate relationship with her brother, Frank. A letter in Ludwick's handwriting confirms he married Frank's sister out of spite because Frank had ended their relationship. He used to be as poor as anyone can be, he had nothing but a rundown bicycle to his name. What he did not lack was being opportunistic, so he wormed himself into the midst of riches with his charm and his wit.

Charl handed me a file which was meant for my father. Or was it more meant for me? It looked like it was immersed in water, like it could have been saved from a sunken pleasure boat. I am guessing.

Ludwick hit a sandbank; doubtless dizzy and disorientated from the overdosage of insulin and alcohol. He must have hit it at a considerable speed because his car was a wreck. The bartender told police investigators that he drank a bit fast. He was killed instantly. My father cut the obituary from the newspaper. He did not say anything when he put it in Ludwick's file. On the cover appeared a big, black "X" and it was shoved back into the deepest, darkest corner of the cabinet. His name would never, ever be uttered again in The Bastion.

Buddy is safe now as are Connie, her sisters and her unborn baby brother.

CHAPTER 22

Five years to the day have gone by since my mother passed away. My father and I went to the rock early and spent some time with her; both of us in silence, just remembering her. It was before the rest of the world stirred, my mother's favorite time of day.

Hannah is playing with Yoda on the carpet. He is a big boy, almost five months old. My mother would have adored him! Yoda was bred especially for us; we waited patiently for his arrival. He was worth every second.

We are in the kitchen. I had the layout of the room changed and I wish I could join their game as unconcerned. It does look a little complicated! Yoda is watching her with his head on his paws. Hannah is showing Yoda a green tennis ball. He watches it but does not take it. Then she hides it behind her back and shows him a yellow one. He watches her, concentrating with multiple frowns on his forehead. Then she shows him a blue one, which she hides with the others.

"Yoda, one two, three," she says, keeping her hands behind her back. It looks as if he understands, not letting his concentration waver, watching her intently. She shows him the yellow ball. Yoda sniffs it but does not take it. Then he sits back on his haunches and emits two sharp little barks. I do not know who looks prouder of the two and I could not love them with more intensity. The happy scene fades from my vision as Hannah shows him the blue ball and he sniffs it again, but I do not hear his answer.

I have a letter on the table counter. I have slit open the others which now lie strewn among the empty yogurt containers and banana peels. It is mostly billing and numerous invitations to open accounts at every conceivable shop.

We have debit orders in place from where all our bills are getting paid. It is a joint account with more than sufficient funds. It is not what is worrying me.

The letter in front of me is addressed to me, Adelaide. It arrived in a blue Croxley envelope amongst the others. The postmark is that of East London and the date stamp yesterdays. The contents are two handwritten pages; all in capital letters and it does not make pleasant reading. I fold it again and take it with the other discarded accounts and invitations, leaving only the slit envelopes to remain in the puddle of milk we spilled.

"You're so quiet," Hannah whispers in my ear; she is hugging me from behind with her arms around my waist. I did not even notice her getting up. Yoda is lying stretched out on the cool kitchen tiles, snoring gently. The colored balls are forgotten next to him. I lay back against her.

"Sorry. I suffer from an easily distracted mind," I answer. "What have I done to Yoda?" I smile, steering the conversation in a different direction.

"Oh, not much!" I sense her smile. "Basic education is quite tiresome, but he is doing excellent for a five-month-old!" She turns me around. "Tracy, don't hide things from me," she says. "We don't do secrets, remember?" I hug her, with my arms and the letters behind her back, feeling like the Judas I am. I can right one wrong by allowing her into a secret.

"Okay" I answer, seeking her mouth for a kiss, "it's a letter."

"ADELAIDE

YOU'VE CONTINUED WITH YOUR LIFE WHILE WE COULDN'T. AS A RESULT, I'M NOW ALONE AND I'M HARDLY COPING. MANY COUNSELING SESSIONS DIDN'T HELP. GOD, WE DID TRY. ALL BECAUSE OF YOU. MAYBE YOU DON'T EVEN RECALL THIS AS IT HAPPENED LONG AGO. IF I KNEW FOR CERTAIN THAT IT BOTHERED YOU, IT WOULD HAVE BROUGHT SOME SMALL REPRIEVE. IT SURE DOESN'T LOOK LIKE IT.

I CAN ONLY BE HEALED IF I AM ABLE TO HURT YOU BACK, IF I CAN AVENGE MYSELF. A DOCTOR TOLD ME TO WRITE YOU A LETTER BUT HE NEVER MENTIONED ACTUALLY MAILING IT. BUT I DID. NOW THERE'S NO TURNING BACK. BESIDES, I WANTED YOU TO KNOW. I HAVE TO ADMIT, I DID FEEL A TINY BIT SORRY FOR YOU WHEN THAT WHORE OF A MOTHER OF YOURS DIED. I GOT TWO BOYS TO SPRAY-PAINT YOUR WALL, I WATCHED YOU SCRUBBING IT OFF AND WISHED YOU DEAD BECAUSE I CAN'T SCRUB MY HEARTACHE AWAY.

IT WAS A USELESS EXERCISE. I DIDN'T FEEL ANY BETTER. YOU LIVE PROTECTIVELY AND WITHOUT ANY FINANCIAL WORRIES. I HAVE NOTHING TO SHOW BUT A BROKEN HOME. IF I WAS MORE IRRESPONSIBLE, I SHOULD HAVE FOLLOWED YOU IN YOUR NEW CAR AND DROVE YOU OFF THE ROAD. BUT I WOULDN'T HAVE BEEN ABLE TO KEEP UP WITH YOU BECAUSE MY CAR IS TOO OLD. I HAVE TO WORK, BLOODY HARD TOO. WHEN I DON'T SHOW UP, I DON'T GET PAID. SO, YOU WERE LUCKY IN ESCAPING.

I BECOME BITTERER OVER TIME. TIME DOESN'T HEAL; I AM A LIVING TESTIMONY OF IT ALTHOUGH I LONG TO BE DEAD. I WANT YOU TO KNOW THAT I'M PLANNING TO REST FOREVER AND SOON. I DON'T CARE IF I DIE BUT NOT BEFORE YOU. IM GOING TO END YOUR LIFE AND I WANT YOU TO KNOW IT. IT CAN BE ANY DAY, IN ANY WAY. ALL I CAN TELL YOU IS THAT IT'LL BE SOON.

IM TIRED. I'M SORE. I'M ALONE. YOU WON'T BE READY TO DIE. IT'S FAR WORSE TO BE ALIVE BUT NOT LIVING. THERE ARE MANY WAYS OF DYING. GOOD."

Hannah is as speechless as I. On reading the letter a second time, I grasp the fervor of it. The hatred of the person who penned the words. I also sense some hesitation. But whoever it is, is determined.

"Tracy? Who could hate you so much?" Hannah asks,

"Just an entire village and then some more," I mouth the familiar, timeworn words. It does not bring us any closer to a solution and it also does not help much in figuring out a plan.

This has nothing to do with Hannah's past but with mine. And my past, my legacy comes with baggage and danger for those I love. It has always been this way.

CHAPTER 23

Miranda took the place of Biddy who eloped. It was a sad day. Miranda is equally professional though and has Ursula in training as a back-up. Smithy took the place of Gregory who unexpectedly passed away. He found himself in front of a car who skipped a red traffic light. He lay in surgery for weeks; just as we thought he would pull through, his condition worsened. After six weeks we received the news of his passing.

I was, amazingly, comfortable with the new additions to the business; now we had to get used to fresh faces behind the cameras.

Today is quite an unusual day. It is my first session as part of an all-girl threesome. We are shooting in my favorite room because of its unusual color combinations. It has white bedding with a purple-colored bedspread and petite bedside lamps with woven reed lampshades in a turquoise and yellow color. A wall-sized black-and-white print depicting a large city at night hangs on the wall above the king-sized bed. My father is watching from a corner of the room. I am pleased to see him. I have watched them often enough; I am proud to show off my skills. Hannah is my main partner. Naturally.

We have Belinda between us. It is her first time with girls and she is as shy as she is inquisitive. I have my pants off but I am wearing a T-shirt and a thong.

Hannah is dressed the same, but Belinda has her breasts naked to the camera.

We are all light-hearted; it is not a serious business but a lot of fun. For the moment sex is our drug, giving us a high. Hannah has two fingers inside of Belinda and I am caressing her, all inside her thong. She is extremely turned on and soaking wet. It makes it easy for Hannah and me to let her peek. Her breathing is coming hard, I kiss her with my tongue slipping in and out of her eager mouth, not allowing her into my own. It is very exhilarating. I know Hannah is as wound-up as me, Hannah opens her to the camera, exposing her by masterfully hooking the restriction of her underwear away with her thumb. Miranda zooms closer onto our faces, we smile with genuine pleasure.

"Don't stop," Belinda begs. She is a lanky brunette with dark eyes and freckles on her nose. She has long hair, like Hannah and I, hanging loosely over her shoulders. Ursula zooms in between her legs where our hands are caressing her, then up towards my face. I smile and give the camera eye a wink. I feel Belinda bucking and whisper to Hannah, "She's almost there," Hannah smiles provocatively; it is all the encouragement Belinda needs. I know the microphone pieces built into our earrings pick up all the sounds. She climaxes with two sharp intakes of breath and a delicious "Ah! Ah!"

"I want to see you do it," Belinda says after catching her breath. She moves out of shot, but we encourage her not to leave the bed. We kiss as lovers in tune with one another. Hannah lifts my T-shirt over my head, stripping herself of hers too. She is on my erect nipples with her tongue, circling it, gently pulling it with her teeth. "I want to, too," Belinda asks. She is busy masturbating hard. Hannah smiles and moves away.

"Sure, suck her," she invites.

I give her my breast, "Hard, suck me hard." Hannah rids herself of her thong, Belinda pulls down mine. I lie down, encouraging Belinda to move down with her mouth between my legs.

Hannah sits over my face; how I love to have control over her! This time I am on the spot, giving and receiving. Belinda is learning fast, stroking me while she opens my lips. I feel myself getting closer to my wake, I hold on to Belinda's head while kneading Hannah's upper leg with the other. I try to keep my tongue inside of her while I prod gently, not wanting to hurt or upset Belinda, who does not know me and may read my actions as an annoyance rather than pleasure. Belinda enters two fingers inside of me: pulling in and out. Then I am there, as close to heaven as I feel certain I will ever be. When I open my eyes, I see Hannah's loving eyes on me as she looks down. "I want you so bad!" I whisper.

"Comme untè," she mouths, sliding down my body, showing Belinda how to get to the classic 'scissoring' position.

I do not know when my father had to leave. I notice his empty chair when the cameras stop rolling and us three girls are trying to find our discarded clothes and underwear, giggling. My father did not have any surgeries or hospital visits booked because he finally took some leave which was long overdue.

He has aged and suddenly, all the girlie fun evaporates. Somewhere out there, just a stones' throw away, Charl keeps watching for stray individuals stalking The Bastion.

Will my father kill yet another dragon for his family?

CHAPTER 24

"Poppet, we've never spoken about the possibility, because it hasn't been necessary. It is a safety precaution built in. In the olden times, families were larger, and daughters married early. There was sure to be a continuous flow of successors. But times change, Honey."

I am trying not to be upset. I have never thought about the likelihood that my father might retire and yet, of course, he must. I am of age and considered a grown up; I must shoulder my responsibility.

"The stipulation in this regard is very clear: a male member must constitute The Bastion's everyday administrative business. Honey, remember, the cog of this wheel is well-oiled. The women rules, men are in supportive roles, only. The age of gallantry in this setup is everlasting. Now you also understand the severe punishment for breaking the Jene Turaq better?"

I do.

"If the devisee is unmarried at the time or underage or in the case of an absent male figure (for example a father), then a record of willing and able members must be consulted, and a choice made from it. Only it. There is such a record, Honey. Remember that your mother's family are a very distinguished and prestigious one. They are the pillars of The Bastion; they have always been supportive, although secretive.

Of one thing you may be sure; you will always have their support. It's time you know about them."

My father is fifty-nine, but he will always be my young father, who could make love so passionately to the woman he loves. He could be tender and gentle to younger women. He is still a very smart man with his dark hair and greying temples. Wrinkles have appeared around his eyes. I know it to be ninety percent laughter and just ten percent worry.

"Daddy, I'm proud of you." I strike up a conversation as we descend the old wooden stairs. "I don't say it often enough, but I love you."

He is still very lean and muscular under his clothes; he often goes to the gym at the private hospital where his theatre is booked. Thinking about it, he has not been active for quite some time.

I am terribly upset to see the tears in his eyes under the dim light of the globe in the little foyer in front of the ancient wooden door. He hugs me, tight and whispers *"Comme Val punt untè, Krak junè Copa."* "I'll love you till death and beyond, my precious girl child."

He steps away, releasing me from his hug and goes down on one knee. I am not shocked because I have been told about this by my mother. He lowers his head, holding his hands behind his back in an act of submission. *"Thesè tura, monè."*

"Get up, knight," I say, stretching out both my hands to take him and help him to his feet.

"Sweet, your father went down on his knee. My heart stopped when he spoke in that old language, and I just knew there would be no other." I recall my mother telling me of my father's proposal for marriage. "Remember this, Sweet; if a man does this, he is ardent to you and it does not have to be a romantic love. Help him rise and you have fashioned a bond stronger than blood. It is unbreakable. Refuse him and you will leave behind a man doomed never to find love."

I wait until my very striking father with our blue eyes looks up, into mine. *"So, me wornè."* "You have my heart" I echo my gorgeous mother's words of so many years ago.

CHAPTER 25

Hannah is not letting me out of her sight, to the extent of her being my constant shadow and I have become very used to seeing her following me. Usually, Yoda is never far behind either. I have slowly moved the ominous letter from my mind; time has misted it over a bit. I cherish Hannah's protectiveness.

I do not realize the grave nature of the threat especially when we are in the safety of The Bastion and Charl has us under his surveillance. He has chased quite a number of homeless men into the dunes, scattering their meager belongings as they ran. He is like a madman! There has not been anybody, yet, who posed a real threat.

I am flicking through our photo album, Hannah and Yoda are downstairs waiting for our pizza delivery. Yoda will dash out of the door when he hears the motorbike, barking excitedly. We always ask for Peter to deliver our orders because Yoda likes him and his parcels very much!

Yoda is a gentle boy in general, but he has his favorites. Peter and his "Beef gumbo special" are two of his most favorite! He will stop short and frown when he sees it is not Peter and erupt in a frenzy of howls, even if the person does not remove the helmet or entice him with the food. If it is not Peter, it is "no go!"

It is a cold Sunday. It has a strange effect on me. My thoughts wander. I am feeling lonely. The Bastion feels strangely devoid of a limb without my father. He has moved to his house on a secluded island in the Caribbean but we are still in regular contact. A very homely lady with the name of Ashley moved in with him. I could not be happier. She is a few years his senior, for a change! I see his face in the pictures, smiling and I wish he did not move that far away. Hannah and I accompanied him on the day he left, leaving The Bastion with its usual business to continue without us. What bliss to be so pleasantly private for a few days.

All my father's tasks are now being taken care of by a distant uncle of mine. Uncle Kaley reassured me via a very official letter of his undivided dedication and of the honor bestowed upon him to become a guardian. My father and I decided on him unanimously; his name was third on the list. Uncle Kaley is much younger than the first two names, which means he would, in theory, be of service for a longer time. He is also closely related to my mother's brother; it brings a comforting reassurance.

I could dismiss him at any time; without explanation if he is not trustworthy or in the case of my own marriage - if I wanted my husband to step in. Of course, in the sad case of his demise, the duties would automatically fall to the next candidate after him.

Copies of all the relevant documents were couriered to him with our private service. I received written confirmation from all the institutions that they had received instructions to redirect all financial and related matters to his address. Copies of it were sent to me simultaneously; it was that easy.

It does not matter that he lives in Scotland and that I have never met him. My father explained it all to me; I need not fret. He could be reached via a special speed-dial number at any time, day, or night.

I drop the album on the bed. We have been reading and making love in "Hannah's abode" as she humorously referred to the rooftop room. We opened the window a little, a cool breeze wafted in. The saltiness in the air is tangible, it tastes condensed. It started raining, a fine smog bringing in moisture from the far reaches of the open expanse which is the ocean. The Bastion's garden's colors flare bright through the misty rain; like beacons out at sea. There are the gentle pink clusters of the *Calodendrum*, the seductive orange-red cubes of the *Burchellia* stars, striking mustard - yellowish *Gazanias*, our *Strelitzia's* remarkable bird-like flowers with its orange petals and even the subdued wild camphor bush wearing her fluffy, dirty-white mothwing -like flowers. Some wildflowers gently sway on their silky stalks, I do not know their names. They sit huddled like children under the green foliage umbrellas of the many indigenous trees and shrubs. It is all so very peaceful; soused and lulled by the dull breaking of the waves along the beach.

I wonder where Hannah and Yoda are. It feels like an unpleasantly long time since they have gone downstairs.

There it is! The unmistakable growl and sputter of the rundown motorbike Peter used for delivering pizzas. The door opens and the security gate slams gently shut, I cannot stand to be alone a second longer and make my way to the bedroom door.

Yoda is howling, I cannot imagine why. Something is very wrong. It is a sound. A horrific sound. It follows shortly after Yoda's howls. Short staccato bursts. Too loud. It shatters the silence and pierces my eardrums. It is a physical hit taking my wind out. It rips into something. My heart stops. The silence is deafening. My legs will not move. The bike is speeding away. Gunshots. Yoda? Frantic, loveable big paws scraping on the wooden door. He is crying.

"No, no, no, no, no, no, no! Hannah? HANNAH! HANNAH! No, no, no, no!"

CHAPTER 25

I run back upstairs taking the steps two at a time. I pull the blanket off the bed and stuff two pillows under my arm. They still feel warm where we sat on them seconds ago. Or was it longer?

"Cold. She will be cold" I keep thinking. When I open the door, Yoda slips in like lightning. He is still crying. "Boy?" I call him. "Here!" I open the refrigerator door with one foot and tip a carton of milk over with my elbow. It spills over the floor, very white. Yoda's body is silvery grey. He discovers the spill and starts licking, his panic hopefully soon forgotten.

Red. Blood. One, two, three. I keep counting, one, two, three, one, two, three. I lift her head gently. Her eyes are open. Loving eyes. Hannah's eyes. Mine. I put the pillow under her head just like I have done many times before. But then there is no blood. She fell backward. I cover her with the blanket. She is wearing her very sexy, tight-fitting jeans. Her feet must not be cold then she will never be warm. No. It is not comfortable for her. I move in behind her and lift the pillow and her head onto my chest. Yes. Now she is okay. I can cradle her like that. I hold on tight.

"Comme untè. Comme untè" I whisper, close to her ear. One, two, three. The fine fog frames us. Picture perfect. Two lovers in a sensual moment would be a textbook description. Like the children hiding under the leaves in the garden.

97

I do not know how long we have been there. I could not let go of her. No. No. I had to be there. I know her. She is mine. She cannot go alone!

There were sirens. People. Pointing. Talking.

Go away. THEY must go!

I do not know what day my father came. I do not know what happened. I only recall Yoda sitting on the kitchen floor with his three colored balls. He sniffed them and barked. Once, then stopped. Twice, then stopped. Three times. There were tears in his eyes, but he was not crying anymore. The tears gushed from my eyes; only I could not cry because I stopped working.

CHAPTER 23

Now, this. I need not anymore. My soul is too drained to carry the yoke. I am just a formless fixation.

We are at home, my father, Yoda and I. It is a business day but there is no business. Faint echoes of laughter and dogs barking seep through the open window. There is something else there too, a memory, a smell. Carefree days of a seaside summer vacation. It is carried upon the still air from the public beach three kilometers away.

"Sweet, look at me," my father prompts, lifting my chin. I do not have any conscious thoughts about my posture,
my behavior, whether I eat or sleep, what I am wearing, eating or drinking.

My father is slowly weaning me from the heavy sedative. He says I will start to feel better. "It wasn't your fault," he says. He is tanned and healthy. He should go home to Ashley. I want him to leave but he is adamant about staying. Perhaps if I play along, he will be convinced and leave on his own. I cannot deceive my father. I must only be honest. Why is it so hard?

I take the newspaper article from him and try to focus unseeing eyes on the words. It is published in today's local edition, 'Nobie News.

Yoda lies content at his feet, his worried, sad eyes on me. He is missing Hannah too and I do not know how to make it better so I give him a smile; I pray that he will understand. We should go swimming, he loves that.

The article reads:

"SELF-CONFESSED MURDERER MURDERED"

Gonubie. 12 December 1992. The small village of Gonubie was shocked to a standstill during the early hours on the 9 December. A mere day before the tragedy, a resident of the village, Mister J. H. de Kok, aged sixty-six handed himself over to the SAPD regional offices in East London. Jacques (SNR) admitted guilt of the murder of Missus Sylvia Crombie. He shot her in front of a friend's home to avenge his son's death (Jacques de Kok, JNR) in 1985. According to reports his son had drowned. The connection is hazy and may now forever remain a mystery. An investigation into the murder at that stage has yielded no credible leads. On 11 December Mister Charl Riewoldt, a renowned local photographer gained access to the holding cells where Mister de Kok was locked up, awaiting trial. He shot Mister de Kok directly and then turned the gun on himself. An investigation is underway to determine the lack of guards on the premises. Doctor J. Khondile, Police Commissioner, told 'Nobie News "he will leave no stone unturned. Tragedies like this are unacceptable and the deaths of two people could have been avoided." He also expressed his condolences to the families of the deceased."

Charl was beyond grief. He came to see me, only after Hannah's memorial service. I remember he slumped onto both his knees in front of my bed. He held his hands as if in prayer while silent tears dripped from his eyes.

"I should have known," he said, begging wordlessly. "The letter was actually so clear, he could have shouted his name from the rooftops! This," he said, his voice cold and calculating, "is unforgivable."

I tried extremely hard to reassure him because if it was anybody's fault, it was mine. I should have made the connection; it was not his fault. I was too drugged, too tired, and too broken to convince him.

"Ki appol ovar," he said, still on his knees. "I've failed you."

When I resurfaced, it was hours later.

My knight went in pursuit of the dragon and found him; detained but still a dragon...

"Honey, Charl doesn't have a family. I do not know how to help you through this other than to be here. We need to take care of him."

I know my father is right. Another memorial service, a reliving of an unspeakable distress. We got hold of Hannah's mother. It was a dreadful experience. She arrived at her daughter's memorial service, stumbling drunk and without a bodice. There was only us. Smithy and Ursula had to physically remove her when she started screaming obscenities. Untruths. Ugly, hurtful words. Words which defiled the person I knew. It hammered in my head like a migraine, and I fainted. But I will do it. For Charl.

"Daddy, you know how much he enjoyed filming

girl-to-girl missionary?" I ask. A tiny flame in my murky world gets lit for my brave knight. My father nods. "Yes. That I do. He said it was the 'freaking coolest thing, like in ever!'" he mimics Charl's accent.

"Let's name it after him."

A smile spreading over his dear face tells me it will be done. There is one more thing.

"Daddy? Please go home. I cannot heal with you here. I need you away from here to be close to you."

My father left during the afternoon and there are no hard feelings between us. I take Yoda down to the beach to go swimming. He is very adept in this exercise, but I never take him in too deep. I want to believe he is as close to Hannah's essence here as I am to her and my mother's. She had Yoda's heart and mine. Hannah left me a tiny piece of herself in Yoda, I will treasure him, always.

We have her kept in the same rock as my mother. My father had another alcove chiseled which we let sealed. The words are simple. "My Hannah. 14 November 1992. *Untè*." Evermore.

I look up to two women, as strong as they were fragile. They, in turn, are keeping watch over me, the mistress of The Bastion.

(Image from Pinterest)

CHAPTER 28

The sedatives' effect is wearing off. I sleep fitfully if at all and during my waking hours I sit and cry with Yoda in my arms. He does his best to lick off the tears and often, this kindness and the mess he leaves on my face, makes me smile.

I spent a lot of time thinking yesterday. I reserved the day for thinking and I have come to a decision. Yoda and I went down to the basement room where I sat and read a lengthy document. It has a list of "inclusives" and "exclusives" and it is difficult to read. I need to know what I am letting myself and my business in for. When I make that phone call, I must be sure. My father has decided on a period of respect for a month, but it has been two weeks and I am ready to go bonkers. I need the drone of activity and humanity around me. For now. For a while. For a few years more.

I finally find what I have been looking for. Under the light of the ceiling-fitted lights, the names take on a life all their own. The personalities of the names on the list seem to communicate themselves through the strokes of the pen which formed the letters. The "a's" speak loudly and aggressively while the "c's and e's" are gentle, and I find the "f's and g's" assertive.

This is a list of women. I have the latest updated list of 1990. It has been done by the mysterious individuals of my mother's family, the true keepers of

The Bastion. I do not have my father to consult; this should be my decision alone. I am taking a few factors into consideration; I cannot make a mistake here. I finally decide. She has experience, is not that old but older than us, she will be shown respect and her name has the characteristics that The Bastion needs.

It is done in less than a minute. Uncle Kaley answers on the second ring. "I'm at your service, Tracy" he says.

"Mare calou galè," I say. "An acting mistress." He does not miss a beat in asking me her name. "Aunt Brix." It takes a few seconds more,

"It will be so," Uncle Kaley says softly. "In two days' time, Tracy. Do you need anything else?" He sounds caring and compassionate, much younger than I know he is.

"No, thank you, Uncle Kaley."

"Boy!" I call Yoda, peacefully sleeping on his side. I am sorry to wake him; he does not get much sleep either because he is forever in my arms when I cry. I see him perk up by the tone of my voice.

"You'll help me, right Yoda?" I ask, stroking his smooth head. He wags his tail excitedly. "We have a few rooms to service, and we'd better prepare my aunt's room too. And when we are done, we will go for a swim. We must also further your education; it has been seriously neglected!"

A sliver of feeling, a little alive, settles in my soul. If it will ever be fully aflame again, I cannot tell. For every discretion recorded in this room; and the punishment that went with it, a lady, a friend, a family, or a lover got hurt first. It may be the way of the world but sometimes death is not punishment enough because it brings so little consolation.

CHAPTER 29

The Bastion settles into its routine again like a donkey trotting along a well-known path with its eyes closed. It knows every bump, every stone, and every uneven surface and if the road turns, it turns with it.

Aunt Brix, aged sixty-seven, settled in like a welcome breeze on a hot summer's day and earned the immediate respect of everybody. Under her care and supervision sessions were booked, the film crew got busy again and days turned into months and months into four years.

Time only stood still for me because nothing changed but the seasons outside my window. I am in some state of hibernation lasting an exceptionally long time. At times I would honor a session by appearing and watching but I have little contact with anybody. It is a preferred state. The people I know so well who have filmed me numerous times, are now avoiding eye contact with me, scared of what they will find there.

I am not always alone in bed. I ask for Jewel sometimes, or even Ursula. I care about it but only to satisfy a minuscule part of me.

Jewel has left her boyfriends; she claims not one of them is worth it and I worry that she shoots them down because of her protectiveness over me. I allow her and when she spontaneously offers her sexual love, I take it. Jewel is in her forties now but an ardent lover and a good friend.

Ursula has lost her shyness. I enjoy teaching her. I have only been with three guys since and only because Aunt Brix invited me. Through her, I met an old acquaintance and a brand-new quest. It would be my last before I retire.

It is like the bodily shock of the sudden contact with bitterly icy water. Your body heat is in such contrast with the cold that it momentarily confuses your mind. Then it registers the cold and starts sending messages; either that of panic or acceptance. I am feeling both.

It has been many years since I last saw him. We were just children then. We have both changed but just on the surface. He was my first. He is tall and muscular, thirty-five years old, two years my senior, to be exact. He wrote his age as "thirty" on his application. He is wearing his age in good form. He has the audacity to visit.

"Aunt Brix," I announce myself.

"Darling, do come in!" she says. She is in her room which used to be my parents'. We have changed the room's ordinary windows to sliding windows which are much wider. It is brighter in the room now, even when the blinds are closed. She has them open.

We moved her bed to the opposite wall, where she could leisurely gaze over the expanse of the ocean. It fills the entire wall; she needs no extra adornments.

Aunt Brix is a very extraordinary woman. I would say she is part human and part goddess. Despite her age, her long hair shows little grey. She wears it in folds which she pins up. Aunt Brix is very slender and dresses in exquisite matching suits, always with matching high heels. Her nails are manicured, and her make-up applied lightly. Only her hands show her age; the skin there is wrinkled with a few tell-tale early liver spots. She is a formidable woman.

I have heard with how much authority she managed a few prickly situations. Aunt Brix does not back away from confrontation and three black crosses appeared on the regularly updated files in her office. I wish I knew more about her.

"Please, don't stand around Tracy. It is your room as much as it is mine!" she says kindly. I feel too inferior to confront her like this, it was easier commanding her to come via Uncle Kaley. To my further mortification, she gets up from her bed where she was lying on her back, reading.

"Ja xe mitre," she says, bowing her upper body slightly. "I'm at your service." I know better than to ask her to refrain from doing it; it is her right.

"Thank you, Aunt," I answer, heading towards a reclining chair which faces the window.

"Please, Aunt, don't sit up, it's a casual visit."

"Where's our boy?" she asks, her eyes searching. Everybody knows Yoda!

"Oh! I left him upstairs, Aunt, he does tend to drool over everything. I didn't want him to make a mess in your room."

She smiles and nods before she resumes her position on the bed. "He's welcome here. Please bring him along next time." We are both facing the windows. "I've always loved the ocean," she says, pointing at it with her hand. "It's powerful, don't you find it so?"

"I do."

A few minutes pass. It is Tuesday, past our filming time without respect.

"Aunt Brix, there's a man I need to be punished. His wrongdoing wasn't upon me."

She does not hesitate. "It will be so. *Stè ne, stè nus.*" Against one, against all.

CHAPTER 30

22 May 2033. There is an electrical storm approaching. The sky is portentously dark and brooding. Lightning cracks the dark surface, still without sound. There is the wind, howling in from the open sea, circling The Bastion like demons searching for a lost soul. It is raining softly; a prelude to what will come. A leaking roof tile permits water to drip onto the carpet, like blood dripping from a severed artery. A lone, blurry light is switched on in the rooftop room. It barely creates a smear when seen from outside. The other rooms' windows show no light; they have been that way for a long time. Some show hairline fractures on their smooth surfaces. Like blind men's eyes they are unseeing. The wooden doors are shut without any hint of an invitation; should they be knocked upon. They are rattling in the wind, old men irritated by the disturbance. A warning to not come close. No one is welcome. Ivies green hands hold The Bastion in its hands; protecting and attempting to preserve what is left of it by supplying a protective shield of intertwined, crisscross running vines over the old brickwork underneath. It is at rest. *"SMEC va Carè"* It is paused.

In a house extremely far away a girl, whose chosen name is Rose, will be coming of age soon. The Bastion is her legacy. The mysterious workings of an ancient family keep the business running. It will always be so. An Uncle Frederique called late last night to introduce Rose. It was time.

There is a figure in the upper room, just a faint silhouette. It is that of the mistress. A car stops briefly at the gate. A door slams glumly before its headlights cleave a path open in the dark road, then disappears in it. An old whore lives there; so, the stories are told. There is a soft knock on the bedroom door before it is opened quietly. "Your three o'clock is here, mistress," the ancient butler announces, smiling.

She turns from her dressing table. "Thank you, Victor" she nods. She was glad when he returned from the island many years ago. He belonged with her.

"What a pretty slip of a woman," she muses, "not unlike me many years ago." She is watching the girl posing in the door. She is wearing heels. Her feet are a little apart. She gets up and goes closer, letting her dressing gown slip from her shoulders, naked underneath. There is a ragged edge of an old stab wound on her hip. She always says, forlornly, it does not belong to her, she only carries it. You will never guess her age as almost fifty. She is indeed still a very noticeable woman.

They are used to one another by now, as they move to the bed, kissing. She kicks off her own shoes, they have diamonds embedded in the soles. And why ever could she not? Her profession is incredibly old! In ancient Greece women had the words "follow me" engraved on the soles of their shoes. The imprints were left in the dust wherever they went.

She has bestowed her girlfriend with many gifts

over the years. A luxury yacht, a house in India, a Lamborghini, a private chauffeur service, various priceless jewelry, and clothing. The only thing she would never give away, though, is her heart.

In the dark kitchen, her father is feeding Yoda pieces of bread and tinned fish. "Come, old friend," he says, touching the dog's silver head. "Let's go to bed. Where are your colored balls, hey?" Yoda wags his tail in answer. "Can you remember four?" Victor chuckles when Yoda rewards him with three little yelps. "I know! Three is good enough! Good boy!" Yoda looks at his master; his eyes are forever searching for another voice he has never quite forgotten.

"This old place will be full of people again soon," Victor muses, leading his way with his fingers against the walls in the dark. "Oh! The Bastion!" he tells Yoda, as he follows. "A dirt- poor bugger like me could only stare at its glory from afar! I had but only empty pockets when I fell in love Yoda."

Outside the storm builds in intensity. It is getting impatient to come to fruition; it blows its breath in sharper, urgent gasps while the lightning finds its target, far out at sea. The aftermath illuminates a sharp pointed rock in the garden, illuminating one of the names briefly. "Charl. 18 July 1950 - 11 December 1992. *Tujè Vare*" Valiant soul. Then it hits with an earthshattering blow, tearing through the fabric of the heavens far above. Seconds before the floods come down; it lights up a framed document in a glass cabinet. Then it starts soaking through the rotten floorboards of the basement where a skeleton lies.

The *Jene Turaq* can never be disobeyed without just penance. Even if it occurred many years ago and even if it was committed to a friend.

Dear Reader

We hope you enjoyed reading our book and found it engaging. Your feedback is very important to us and to future readers.

We would greatly appreciate it if you could take a few moments to write a review on Amazon. Your opinion helps others make informed decisions and helps us better understand what our readers value.

Thank you very much for your support!

Kind regards

The Malherbe Team